What the cri

FIVE HEARTS! "...This is a beautifully written new take on some very old Greek myths. The love and sex between Violet and Nick is beautiful intense and so yummy that you will be panting for more. I thoroughly enjoyed this beautiful story and highly recommend it to anyone that enjoys a good love story."

-Lisa Wine for The Romance Studio

FIVE HEARTS "...Ms. Starr's writing brings out the interactions between these two so realistically that one can actually see Nick become human again. This is definitely one book that is necessary to read for its beautiful scenes and of course seeing a mythological god come to life and explore his wild erotic side."

-Melinda of Love Romances

FOUR STARS "...In Violet Among The Roses, much off the tale focuses on Narcissus's sexual awakening; his exploration of love, both the physical and emotional, is enlightening...the characters' development is on point, and the small amount of secondary characters add flavor."

-Susan Mobley of Romantic Times Book Club

ELLORA'S CAVE
ROMANTICA PUBLISHING

VIOLET AMONG THE ROSES
An Ellora's Cave Publication, July 2004

Ellora's Cave Publishing, Inc.
PO Box 787
Hudson, OH 44236-0787

ISBN 1-84360-892-8
ISBN MS Reader (LIT) ISBN # 1-84360-668-2 October 2003
Other available formats (no ISBNs are assigned):
Adobe (PDF), Rocketbook (RB), Mobipocket (PRC) & HTML

Edited by RAELENE GORLINSKY
Cover art by NATHALIE MOORE.

VIOLET AMONG THE ROSES

By Cricket Starr

Chapter One

The short, squat gardener halted his work with the clippers and straightened from the hedge. Running his hand through his thinning gray hair, his eyes narrowed in consternation. "Edgar, you notice anything funny about that statue?"

His partner, a tall, spare man in his early fifties, sat up and leaned back on his heels, momentarily forgetting the dandelion plant in his hand. He peered beneath the brim of his NYC pitcher's cap at the center of the flowerbed, where a gleaming figure perched on a two-foot high pedestal.

The fountain was the showpiece of the park, a genuine French sculpture made of white marble, the figure of a young man crouched by a pool; the water flowed in from the side so the surface was always mirror smooth. He'd been carved with beautifully defined muscles, barely covered by the simple garment that flowed from one shoulder and wrapped around his waist for modesty. Marble sprigs of tiny flowers surrounded his hard thighs and bare feet, as well as lining the edge of the basin.

Concerned, Edgar peered closely at the figure. He saw no cracks in the marble or unusual wear of the glossy surface. No dirt even. The thing looked fine. "Can't say that I do, Chauncey. What's wrong with it?"

His partner continued to stare. "Well, that's supposed to be Narcissus, right?"

Edgar glanced at the plaque on the pedestal. "Right..."

"And Narcissus was that Greek dude that was so stupid that he fell in love with his own reflection in a pool, right?"

"Yeah..." Edgar looked at the figure. "Hey, I see what you mean. The statue isn't staring into the water anymore."

"That's what I mean. He's looking over there." Chauncey indicated the direction with his prominent chin. "At that bench."

Both men examined the empty park bench, clearly the object of the statue's attention. Made of smooth concrete and partially obscured by rose bushes that even this late in the fall sported blossoms of various hues, it was in a beautiful location, one well-known to both the public park gardeners and the public itself as an ideally secluded place for lovers to meet.

Edgar scratched his unshaven chin, pondering the situation. It sure did look like the statue had moved its head. Then he shrugged. "Probably one of those art folks from the city came in and switched out the statue." He returned his attention to the weed in his hand, pulling it with a grunt.

Nodding slowly in satisfaction, Chauncey returned to trimming the hedge that bordered the fountain. That had to be the answer. After all, it wasn't like the statue could actually move.

* * * * *

The gardeners finished their work and moved to another area of the park, leaving the marble figure alone to continue his steadfast observations, staring at the empty bench on the other side of the narrow gravel path. During the next two hours, he was able to view a number of the interactions the bench was famous for, beginning with a young nurse with her infant charge, who met a dashing young policeman for a quick tête-à-tête in the middle of the morning. While the baby napped, the pair enjoyed a quick cuddle, sitting as close as the bench and propriety allowed.

Afterwards a man in a business suit met a charming young woman in a waitress uniform, on break from a nearby coffee shop. The continual ringing of the man's cell phone spoiled their idyll, until he turned it off for the remainder of their stay.

Lunch brought a pair of workers from the nearby office park. They spent as much time nibbling each other as they did the sandwiches in their brown paper bags.

In the afternoon, a crowd of children played games around the bench and ran along the path to and from the nearby playground. Their presence, while delightful, discouraged any would-be lovers. Only in the late afternoon, after the juvenile crowd had disappeared in the directions of their homes, did an elderly couple arrive. Bundled up in heavy coats against the afternoon chill, they wandered the narrow path and spent a few moments cuddling on the bench. Their faces might have been covered in wrinkles, but there was no age in the soft loving whispers the pair shared.

Through it all, the statue kept his quiet vigil, patient as only stone can be.

It was very late in the day when the final visitor to the bench arrived. In the early evening stillness, there was the sound of a pair of soft-soled shoes shuffling down the gravel path. The footsteps gave the impression of either great age—or great sadness.

A woman came into sight. Young, maybe twenty-eight, scarcely the oldster she might have been taken for. Her head was covered with mouse-brown hair in a nondescript cut, her body dressed in oversized, stone-washed jeans and a baggy dark green sweatshirt, the front of which boasted an array of cheerful daisies, a decided contrast to the woe-be-gone expression of its owner.

Like a woman twice her age, she carefully lowered herself onto the bench. For a moment she merely sat there, gazing with unseeing eyes in the direction of the statue across the path. Then she buried her head in her hands and the twilight stillness was broken by her soft sobbing grief.

Inaudible to human ears, a quiet chant began, a male voice, deep and sweet, reciting in a language from long ago:

"Oh mighty Aphrodite, Goddess of Beauty,

Thou art love,

Thou art fire,

Thou art all a man might desire.

Aphrodite, fairest of goddesses,

Bringer of passion,

Splendid and sweet,

Goddess of Beauty, hear my plea."

Next to the fountain a whirlwind formed, picking up dirt and fallen leaves, collecting petals from the surrounding flowers. It turned, twisted, rising high into the form of a human being, and settled back to earth. When the dust cleared, a woman stood.

She was beautiful. The most beautiful woman imaginable, hair like a silver and gold curtain down her back, eyes the color of the purest sapphires. Her skin was like alabaster, tinged with rosy pinks that put the fairest peach to shame. The Goddess of Beauty indeed—Aphrodite, fairest of the ancients.

The goddess leaned against the basin of the fountain and spoke to the statue, witness to the sobbing figure with his frozen stare.

"Pretty words, Narcissus, very pretty indeed. And so *sincere...*" Her laugh rippled like the water trickling into the basin. She glanced over at the despondent form on the bench and folded her arms, one delicately arched eyebrow displaying her amusement.

"Such a flattering speech. I wonder what prompts you to make it?"

"Beautiful Lady. I...I merely wanted to see you, of course."

"You merely wanted me to see this, you mean." The goddess's eyes ran over the still-crying figure and their ironic amusement developed into true sympathy. "She does seem rather upset."

"Her name is Violet Smith. Her family is gone, her cat dead, her boyfriend dumped her, and last week she lost her job. Yes...she's upset."

The goddess glanced back at the figure on the pedestal. "How do you know all this? It was just a day ago that I granted your wish to move your head to spy on that bench."

"I know this because the bastard she's been living with broke up with her last week on that bench—after she told him about losing her job. It seems that the only reason he was with her in the first place was because she had a good income and could support him."

"That's a shame, Narcissus, but what would you have me do about it?" Aphrodite tapped her slender finger on the side of her cheek. "I could turn the selfish brute into a statue, I suppose, but that would hardly help her."

"Well, I was thinking." Narcissus's voice grew tentative. "You remember that offer you made? To give me the opportunity to learn about love?"

The goddess clapped her hands together in delight. "You wish to take me up on that after so many centuries?" She looked thoughtful for a moment. "There is this one nymph I've been training. She'd be an excellent instructor…"

Carefully, Narcissus cleared his throat. "Blessed goddess, lovely as I'm sure your fair one is…I had someone else in mind."

Again the goddess's attention was diverted to the sobbing figure among the roses, her expression this time of disbelief. She pointed one long elegant finger. "You would prefer *that* to one of my special protégés?"

"Well…yes."

"Why?"

"Mighty Aphrodite, you know the kind of learning I want. While I want to understand the physical, I want more than that…I want to know about the emotional as well."

A glint of a smile graced the perfect lips. "This from the man who drove away my favorite nymph when all she wanted was a taste of your gorgeous body?"

His voice turned desperate. "Please, great lady. You know I was very young and didn't understand what your fair one offered me. I wish to learn about that now, but I want the other as well. I want to know about love."

The great goddess turned to the unfortunate young woman on the bench and considered her with more interest. A speculative gleam filled her eyes. "A woman who inspires love in the man who could only love himself. Fascinating. I find this warrants further study."

She returned her attention to the statue. "You wish to become human, so that you can learn about love from a human woman." One elegant hand pointed to Violet, a hint of bemused wonder in her voice. "*That* woman."

"Yes, Mighty Goddess."

"Why her?"

"She looked at me—it's a long story, Sweet Goddess."

Interest tinged Aphrodite's fair features. With an infinitely graceful movement she settled on the edge of the fountain. Checking her reflection in the mirrored surface, she tucked a long strand of hair behind one perfectly shaped ear. Satisfied, she dipped her fingers in the pool, and watched the ripples form and bounce off the far edge. "I have much time, Narcissus, as do you. Tell me this story of yours."

The statue would have sighed if he could. He continued to stare at the woman on the bench; his expression might have been frozen, but his voice emoted enough to make up for it. All he wanted at the moment was to be able to comfort sweet Violet, to show her that someone cared for her—even if that someone was made of stone. He could do it if he was human, but the only way he could become human was to acquire the goddess's sympathy.

"My story begins many years ago. She's been coming to this park since she was a little girl. Most of the time, I don't notice the people, particularly the children. They move too fast, don't stay in one place long enough. But Violet was different." He remembered that difference. It had been her stillness that he'd noticed.

"When I was looking into the pool, I would see my reflection, but I'd also see some of the sky, occasionally a bird, or the leaves on the trees. Sometimes a flower would float in the water." His voice grew wistful. "I liked that, when I could see something besides my own face."

"But it's such a beautiful face, Narcissus," the goddess teased.

Somehow he did manage a sigh. "I've been staring at it for two hundred years, Majesty. I'd be happy not to ever see it again."

"I'll keep that in mind." Her amused response almost sounded like a threat and for a moment the statue wondered if what he was doing was such a great idea. Aphrodite was known for her "practical jokes". But she was also known for her enjoyment of a good love story and it seemed a good idea to get back to his.

"One day a young girl stuck her head over the pool, to stare into my reflected face. Others had done that, but she stayed that way for a long time, studying me. I noticed her." His voice faltered. "For the first time, someone looked into my eyes. She tried to say my name, but couldn't manage the S's so she decided to call me 'Nick'. Someone called her name, 'Violet'—and she ran away. Ever since then when she's come to the park, she's come to my pool and talked to me. She told me her secrets. She called me her friend.

"A few years ago, Violet told me that her parents died, and her tears fell in the water beneath me. She's told me other things as well. Only when she began seeing this man did she stop visiting me. I've missed her..." His voice trailed off.

"And now that man has deserted her and you wish to take his place?"

His voice was quiet, resigned. "I know you can't do that, Aphrodite. I'm here to serve punishment, and to release me from it would be against the rules the gods set down. But I was wondering if you could maybe bend the rules a bit. For just a little while."

"Just a little while?" The goddess pondered that. "Perhaps I could. A few hours...but no, that wouldn't be long enough. Overnight perhaps?"

"One night?" Disappointment touched him. "That would be enough time for sex but for more..."

Aphrodite pursed her exquisite lips. "You have a point. To really understand love takes time. Two nights, then, and the day between. From dusk today until dawn on the next. That would be enough time for you to comfort her, and to learn what you want to know about love."

Joy leapt in his voice. "Oh, Aphrodite, if you could, I would be so eternally grateful. I'd worship you forever."

Again her face bore a secret amusement. "Be very careful what you promise, say, or even think, Narcissus. I might hold you to any or all of it."

Chapter Two

Aphrodite raised her hand and placed it on his head. "Come to life, Narcissus, as you were once before. Be of carved stone no longer, but living flesh and blood."

A hush filled the air around them, then a warm breeze blew into the garden and around the man of stone. It centered on the goddess' hand, lightly touching the stone hair. Slowly color seeped into it, a rich black flowing away from her palm, into the curls below. As she pressed, they became soft. She pulled her hand away and stood back to watch, eyes twinkling in amusement in the near dark.

The transformation picked up speed. The texture of the face, the ears and neck changed, softened, took up color, a rich light tan that spread downward across his chest into his torso, from there to his arms and legs. The feet and hands, pressing against the marble of the fountain basin, took on color, and the digits moved, clenched against the stone surface.

Even the carved fabric of his garment changed, took on a deep brown hue and became the simple peasant garment the sculptor had envisioned Narcissus wearing in life. It fluttered in the soft breeze that also ruffled his newly created hair.

His face changed, dark eyebrows and eyelashes forming against the tan skin, and when he blinked, the irises of his eyes changed from white to a rich brown. Lips took on a deep shade of rose and softened, and the tip of a tongue appeared in the opening, red against the white of his teeth, the only thing left that retained the perfect color of the original marble.

His chest heaved and his mouth opened further, eyes widening in the process. For a moment he held his breath, then he breathed out slowly. Stiffly at first, then with more grace, he tilted his head to move his stare to the goddess standing nearby.

The perfect tongue licked his lips and he opened his mouth to speak, but found it hard to make the words form. "Mighty One."

He would have fallen off his perch, but she placed a hand on his elbow and helped him down, his newly formed muscles not quite under his command as yet. Standing on the ground, he leaned against the fountain pedestal, taking deep breaths.

"I'm alive," he finally managed. He touched his face and stared at his hands in wonder. Fingers clutched into a fist, then relaxed, spread out. A smile formed on his perfectly made lips. "It's a miracle."

"That's what goddesses do, Narcissus, perform miracles." She gazed at him, her amusement growing, even as she admired him. "You are even better looking than I expected. But remember, this is temporary only. Just until dawn the day after tomorrow. You must return to the fountain then."

"I understand." He turned his attention to the woman seated on the bench just yards away, so preoccupied with her sorrow that she hadn't noticed the statue coming to life. "It will be worth it," he murmured under his breath.

"Narcissus, there is one thing I want to point out. Your Violet may not be as easy to convince to be your teacher as you might expect. The women of this time aren't gullible. She may not even believe you when you tell her who you are."

The newly made man hesitated. Aphrodite did have a point. He'd witnessed thousands of encounters in the park that had gone badly, and it was important that, if this one were to succeed, he start off right.

He turned a coaxing smile on the goddess. "I suspect if I had help, Violet would believe me. I bet I could even make her love me."

The goddess looked outraged. "Are you suggesting that I call in my son, Eros, and that ridiculous bow and arrow of his just so that you can get laid?"

Narcissus waved his hands in immediate negation. "No, of course not, Great One. I apologize that you misunderstood me. As I said, it's not just sex I want. I want to love Violet and earn her love in return. But if I can't get her to talk to me, or if she won't even let me get close to her…"

His plaintive tone must have appeased her. Aphrodite shook her head. "Very well, Narcissus, I'll do this. I'll make certain she believes you. She's sure to be attracted to you…" Here Aphrodite gave him a long lascivious look that left his new skin heated in a full-blown blush. "I'll just see to it that she's inclined to act on that attraction. Anything else will be left up to you, but if you need any inspiration, just call me."

She paused then gave him a little mischievous smile. "Oh, and one more thing…" Reaching for him, she grasped his privates and gave them a gentle squeeze. The resulting hardness in his penis made him gasp aloud.

When she released him, the stiffness fled and he was left with a mild throbbing along his shaft and in his balls.

"You'll have no trouble keeping that at attention tonight or tomorrow." She winked. "Let's just say that you'll be making up for the last three thousand years."

Barely able to focus on her words, Narcissus turned to stare at Violet, still oblivious to them in spite of their conversation. Apparently Aphrodite had shielded them from view. The sight of Violet's forlorn figure sent a rush of longing through him, some of it lingering in his still tingling rod, which jerked under his simple robe.

As if understanding she no longer held his attention, Aphrodite threw up her hands. "Go now and learn about love, Narcissus. Make my help worthwhile."

Narcissus bent to one knee and clasped her perfect hand. "Thank you, Goddess, for everything."

Smiling, she stepped back. The wind came up again and whirled around her form, catching her hair and gown in its excitement. Leaves and dust blew into a cloud that hid her from view, and when it dispersed she was gone.

* * * * *

"Violet?"

The soft-spoken sound of her name drew Violet's attention into the present, away from the desolation of her life. She was in the park, her favorite place in the world, the place she most often came when life was bleakest.

No one knew she was here. How would someone know her name? Through her tears, she blinked, trying to make sense of the man standing before her. The first things she saw were warm brown eyes, framed by lush black lashes, the kind of lashes a woman would die to have—and usually showed up on her younger brother. On this man, they looked good.

The rest of his face wasn't bad either. Perfect cheeks, thick, soft lips, a nose long and straight and prominent enough to keep him from looking feminine. A nice face, handsome.

The expression in his beautiful eyes was one of sweet anxiety. What was that handsome face doing, staring into hers with such impassioned concern? And how did this gorgeous man know her name?

She widened her field of vision to take in the rest of him, and shock overcame the rest of her questions. The man was practically naked! A thin skirt of fabric was wrapped around his waist, providing him with a minimum of modesty, one long triangle rising to partially cover his well-built chest. Barefoot, bare-armed, and practically bare-chested—it was mid-fall, and she shouldn't even be out here without a coat. Just looking at him gave her a chill.

Violet pointed to what constituted his clothing. "Aren't you cold?"

He blinked at her and glanced down. Goose bumps formed on his exposed skin and he rubbed one finger along them. A quiet laugh escaped him. "I guess I am. It's been so long since I had a body, I didn't recognize the sensation." To her dismay, he took a seat on the bench next to her.

So long since he had a body? Violet edged away from him. Clearly the man wasn't all there... although the part present certainly was impressive. "What do you want?"

He smiled revealing perfect teeth, so white they gleamed even in the soft twilight. "I wanted to talk to you, Violet."

"Do I know you?"

His smile became hesitant. "In a way. You call me Nick."

Violet's brow wrinkled in confusion. Nick? Who did she know named Nick? No one, no one at all. It was a pet name she'd always liked. Surely she would remember someone who carried that name. She ran her eyes along his chest again.

Surely she would remember a man who looked like this!

On the other hand…wait a minute, that's what she called the…she glanced over at the middle of the garden, spied the empty pedestal, and her jaw dropped.

Fear sending tiny trembles along her spine, she returned her stare to the man sitting next to her.

The half-naked man sitting next to her.

The half-naked man who resembled, and was dressed like, her favorite statue.

He seemed to read her expression, understand what was wrong. "Yes, Violet. That's where I was." His voice was soft, soothing. It was all she could do to resist being carried away by it—but resist she did.

He glanced back at the fountain. "I was there a long time. You were the only one who ever talked to me."

"What—why—how?"

"How is it I'm not a statue? I asked the goddess Aphrodite to turn me into a real man. She did it, but only for a few hours. Until two days from now." A look of sadness crossed his face. "Then I must return."

"Why?" She seemed to be having trouble with anything other than one-word questions. Fortunately Nick wasn't having trouble understanding her.

"Why did I want to become real? That's a little hard to explain." He sighed. "The goddess and I go way back. Aphrodite is the embodiment of physical love, and I'm the symbol of self-absorption. When I was a young, untried youth, one of her favorite nymphs fell in love with me. She followed me everywhere and tried to seduce me, but I wouldn't give her what she wanted. Finally she got fed up and complained to the goddess, who spoke with her son. She got Eros to hit me with an arrow just as I was passing a smooth pond."

She wasn't all that familiar with Greek mythology, but Violet had heard this story and knew what happened next. For once she was able to put a sentence together. "You saw your reflection and fell in love with yourself, thinking it was another person."

If anything the blush on his cheeks made him look more adorable. It was all Violet could do to resist patting his reddened face.

"I spent every minute I could gazing at myself, obsessed with my own reflection. Eventually I became ill, unwilling to leave the pond long enough to eat or rest. Even as I wasted away, I couldn't resist wanting what I couldn't have. I died there, the thing I loved best just outside my reach."

A wave of sympathy passed through Violet, and she did reach for and take his hand. Nick's eyes widened at her touch and he stared in wonder at their clasped hands until Violet realized what she was doing and pulled away.

Regret colored his face as he continued his story. "After I died, my spirit became caught up in the world of the gods, and I existed as a disembodied spirit among them. I never gave them the reverence they felt they were entitled to—after the dirty trick played on me, why should I? They may be the embodiment of human emotions and appetites, but that didn't make them true gods, not to me.

"Take Aphrodite, for example. A long time ago the goddess told me that if I ever experienced sex, I'd end up worshiping her. So long as I didn't have a body there wasn't much chance of that, so I didn't take it seriously. I even told her that."

He shook his head, as if disgusted at his own stupidity at tweaking the nose of a powerful immortal being. "But then she inspired a sculptor to carve my statue so perfectly that the marble actually captured my spirit and made me part of the physical world again. I was able to see, hear, and, to some extent, feel. And since I could see and feel, I learned to want."

Nick reached out a tentative hand and lightly stroked the back of hers. Violet wanted to pull it away, but before she could, he withdrew. She stared at the place he touched, still feeling that gentle contact, almost bereft that it was gone.

Lifting her head, she stared into his eyes and once more fell under the spell of those warm brown orbs.

"Want what?"

"What do I want? I told you, I wanted to speak to you." He hesitated. "You were hurting, I wanted to help. Make you feel better."

"How?"

He reached out to her, clasping her upper arms and pulling her toward him. "By loving you, sweet Violet."

Sensibility snapped back in the instant. Violet placed a hand in the center of his chest, ignoring the odd thrill the contact brought her. Finally, she managed to find her tongue.

"So, let me get this straight. You are the statue I've been calling Nick, the one from the fountain. You're alive because you asked a goddess, Afrodady, to make you human, so you could make me feel better. By loving me."

"Aphrodite."

"What?"

"A-phro-di-te," he said, enunciating each syllable carefully. "That's the goddess' name. You don't want to get that wrong, she's easily riled. Otherwise, I think you have it."

"Right." It was such a shame. He was such a nice looking mental patient. "I have to be going now."

He blinked, realization showed in his face. "You don't believe me?"

Avoiding the hurt look he was giving her, Violet stood, prepared to run if necessary. For the first time she realized how quiet the park was. No one was about but the pair of them.

"Listen, I'm sure someone will come get you soon. If you like, I'll call them when I get home." Even if he didn't like, she was going to call the authorities. She backed down the path, wary of pursuit.

He made no move toward her. "Charlie...that was your cat."

"What?" Oh great, I'm back to single-word sentences again.

"Your cat," he continued. "Charlie. He ran away two weeks ago and was hit by a car. It made you cry."

She took her time, allowed the words to form slowly. "How did you know about that? I haven't told anyone…"

"You told me. You came to the fountain and whispered it to me." The eyes he raised to her were clear, intelligent, no sign of lunacy. "You've always done that, since you were a child, come to me and told me your secrets, what was right and wrong in your life. You told me all the things you didn't dare tell another."

She froze on the spot. Glancing behind her, she once again took in the empty pedestal of the fountain. Could it be? He was right, she had told the statue her troubles, most recently the one about Charlie's death. She hadn't worked her way up to telling him about Gary. That was one of the reasons she was here tonight.

Nick rose from the bench and took a step toward her. "I'm not going to hurt you, Violet. All I want is to help."

"Help how?" At last some improvement—at least that was two words.

"By showing you love. The men you've been with, they haven't done that."

Outraged, Violet stood her ground. "How do you know that?"

He reached out, grabbed her hand. Pulling her to him, he traced the edge of her face. His touch made her uncertain, giddy, and the sensation disarmed her indignation.

"I know, Violet. I know because you'd never have stayed with someone like Gary if you'd ever known true passion."

Breathless, she tried to defend herself. "What do you know about Gary?"

"Enough. I've been here when you've met him, when he's talked to you. I heard what happened between you." One of his arms snaked across her back, pulling her close to him. "Take me home with you. I promise I'll show you what you've been missing." His voice was a dark sensual purr.

Caught between common sense and the rest of her senses, Violet struggled with what to do. Part of her believed Nick, or at least believed his claim that he'd make her forget Gary. Just having Nick's arm around her was making it hard to picture Gary's face.

The other part told her that she'd be crazy to invite a total stranger home and that they didn't get much stranger than Nick, a man claiming to be a statue who'd come alive through the actions of a Greek goddess.

She waited so long to make up her mind that Nick had the opportunity to lean forward, his lips aiming for hers. Violet felt the touch of those soft lips on her own, his perfect tongue seeking the opening to her mouth with shy confidence, slipping silky smooth along her teeth. She responded in a way she couldn't remember ever doing before, her mouth softening under the gentle plying of his, her tongue meeting his, thrust for thrust in simple abandon.

It wasn't the kiss of a stranger. He kissed her as if he had a right to it, as if they'd kissed thousands of times in the past, so well did his lips know hers. Every argument she had came undone in the midst of that gentle kiss.

Kiss? No, it wasn't just a kiss, certainly unlike any kiss she'd ever known. It was less a meeting of lips than a reunion of two souls who'd once been ripped apart and who'd now found each other at last. It was the sweetest and most passionate thing she'd ever experienced. She pulled back from him and saw in his wide dark-rimmed eyes the same wonder.

The sky overhead seemed to reflect her own mixed emotions, taking the debate within her into its charge. In just in the short time they'd been kissing, clouds had formed in the clear sky, dark and ominous. With a flash of light and answering rumble, the darkened heavens opened up and within moments rain drenched the area, soaking through Violet's sweatshirt and what little clothing Nick wore.

She shuddered violently from the sudden cold.

Or was it Nick's kiss?

Ignoring the little voice that said it was more the latter than the former, Violet grabbed his hand. She peered at him through the hair dripping into her face. "I guess you better come home with me."

Chapter Three

Violet lived in a house just a couple of blocks from the park. Small, with red brick siding, a deep front porch, and white picket fence, it held a pair of bedrooms, single bath, living room with attached dining area, and kitchen. Inherited from her folks, the place was warm and cozy, and moreover, it was dry.

After rushing through the rain, home looked even better than usual. With an uncharacteristic unconcern about allowing a stranger into her home, Violet opened the door and let them both inside, bolting the lock against the rain and dark behind them.

Nick behaved as if he'd never been inside a house before. Violet watched as he wandered around the place, examining even the most commonplace twenty-first century fixtures with wonder. When she turned the lights on, he startled and stared, as if magic lived in the walls and the living room lamps.

If he wasn't a man from another century, he certainly knew how to behave like one. Nick loved the switch that controlled the wall outlets, flicking it on and off with a fascination she found disturbing. When he was done with the lights, he tried the furniture in the room, sitting on the chairs and the coffee table. He tested the soft cushions on the couch, and checked out the bookcase and its books with positive glee.

As she watched him explore the room's furnishings, Violet also found it disturbing how his clothes molded to his body when wet. The man was altogether too good-looking and the sight of him stirred up senses she'd learned to ignore living with Gary.

Finally she couldn't take it any longer. "You need something dry," she said and fled for her bedroom. Peeling her own rain-soaked clothing off and tossing them into a corner, she pulled on her heavy, dark-blue corduroy robe, luxuriating in its warmth. In spite of the robe's comfort she was shivering, from the rain, or shock—which she couldn't tell.

Violet sat on the bed, wondering what to do. A deep shudder ran through her. She needed a warm bath, but she couldn't let Nick run around in his wet clothes and catch cold. First she needed to find something for him to wear.

Searching through the clothes Gary had left, she found a pair of boxers and a large T-shirt. The men were of a similar size, if not shape; they would fit Nick.

She turned to find that he, too, had decided his wet clothing was a problem. Nick stood in the doorway, his sodden outfit no longer clinging to his body, but dangling from one hand. "It was uncomfortable," he explained, checking out her robe with obvious interest.

Oh...my...goodness. The sculptor responsible for Nick's form had been a genius with a wonderful imagination. Naked, the former man of stone was absolutely gorgeous, all long molded muscles and smooth skin. And his privates!

Wow. It really had been a shame to cover those with such an ugly garment. For a moment Violet hefted Gary's hideous cast-off boxer shorts and questioned why she wanted to do just that.

Nope. That was definitely going in the wrong direction. "Here." Violet shoved the clothes into his arms before she could allow herself any further thoughts on the matter. What was wrong with her, contemplating giving the man run of her house in all his nude glory?

He examined her offering with no little disdain, holding up the boxers. His nose wrinkled. "What do I want these for?"

"To cover up." She pointed to the most ambitious evidence of the sculptor's art. "You don't want to run around with your penis hanging out."

She felt his gaze follow her down the hall as she headed for the bathroom, and a hot flush replaced the chills she'd been experiencing. Perhaps she needed a cold shower instead of a warm soothing bath.

* * * * *

Wearing the shirt and shorts she'd given him, Nick searched for Violet, and found that she'd secluded herself in the little room she'd called a bathroom when she'd given him a tour of her house on first arrival.

It was unlike any bathing room he'd ever seen, with fine white porcelain fixtures, only two of which he'd immediately understood. The bathing tub was obvious, particularly since the room took its name from it, and the smaller basin at waist height was clearly to cover the cleansing of smaller areas like face and hands.

The one that looked like a seat, with a handle that poured water into a pot underneath—he had suspicions about the use of that fixture. He'd find out later if he was right.

But now he paused in the hallway outside the closed door, listening to the sound of water running into the bathing tub. The air that slipped through the cracks around the door carried the smell of some sweet oil that Violet must have added. It was a lovely scent, that of pine needles.

In the instant he was taken back to his youth, running through the forests near Athens, encountering the supernatural folks that dwelled there—the satyrs, the dryads, the gods and goddesses, and sons and daughters of the same. He remembered the nymphs who'd chased him for his beauty, offering their bodies for games he hadn't wanted to play—until now.

In his mind he pictured the forest near the quiet pool where he'd seen his reflection, and done in by one nymph's evil wish and Eros's arrow, had fallen hopelessly in love with the one person he could never really have. Himself.

He might call himself "Nick", but he was still Narcissus, the man who loved only himself. Guilt filled him, and concern. Did he really have something to offer a wounded soul like Violet?

For a moment he considered leaving and returning to the park, promising the goddess some other entertainment instead. It would be better not to continue if through his selfish nature he ended up hurting Violet instead of helping her.

But no. The goddess had only given him this one opportunity to experience love. If he quit now, he'd simply find himself made of marble once more, and the goddess would never let him hear the end of it. He'd never have another chance to love Violet—she would be lost to him forever.

From inside the door, he heard a soft sound of fabric hitting the tile floor, followed by one gentle splash, then another. He closed his eyes, imagined the reality behind the sounds, Violet undressing, removing the robe and dropping it, revealing her luscious body beneath. He imagined her naked form entering the tub, one foot then the other, then the slosh of displaced water as she slid all the way in. He heard another sound—a heartfelt sigh, almost a moan, and nearly groaned himself in sympathy.

Violet was in the tub, naked and alone.

A stirring within him started, overwhelming and urgent, just as it had when the goddess had touched him. He opened the boxers and glanced down to see his penis now boasted twice the size it had previously. Unconscious of what he was doing, he reached to fondle the affected part. The feeling was excruciatingly lovely and the size grew even more.

Wow. It had been a very long time since he'd been hard there…well, he'd been hard when he was made of stone, but it hadn't been the same thing. He'd almost forgotten what having an erection felt like.

Nick tried the door and found it unlocked. Cautiously slipping through, he entered the steam-filled room. The view was hazy, not unlike the park when it was enveloped in an early hour fog. But this was warm, inviting, not cold and clammy.

For a moment he pictured himself back on his pedestal, enshrouded in a fog, and the image dismayed him. It was wonderful to be able to move around, experience warmth and comfort.

Violet had turned off the overhead lanterns in the room, the ones controlled by the little switch by the door. Near the tub a pair of fat, white, cherry-scented candles provided the only light.

He closed the door and, moving cautiously, careful not to be seen or heard, navigated through the mist toward the bulky tub where he could hear Violet splashing.

Her back was to him, her long brown hair piled haphazardly on the top of her head, fastened with a large golden clip, not for fashion's sake but simply to keep it out of the water. Nick thought the effect of her brown curls so carelessly secured was more erotic than the most elaborately styled hairdo. A single pull and her hair would tumble down her back and across her shoulders.

The nape of her neck was left bare, long, lovely, perfect for nibbling on. He longed to run his teeth and tongue down that expanse and taste the sweetness of Violet's skin.

She still hadn't noticed him. Moving slowly and as quietly as he could, he approached closer, kneeling by the edge of the tub. He tapped her on the shoulder. "That looks nice. Can I join you?"

Her abrupt turn displaced a wave of water from the tub onto him, soaking his shorts and T-shirt. The wet fabric clung to him in a most uncomfortable fashion, particularly on his engorged shaft.

One thing about the real world—it was certainly easy to get wet! As a statue he'd stood in the rain thousands of times, and never felt it at all, and now he'd been soaked twice in just an hour. Quickly Nick slipped out of the sodden clothes and tossed them aside.

She'd scooted away from him, leaving room in the tub behind her. Nick took advantage of it, entering the water as smoothly as a seal to the sea. Oh, it was heavenly sitting in such warm water! In his home in Athens he'd taken more baths in cold ponds than he'd liked, and he'd watched the gods with astonishment when they acquired hot pools around the time of the Romans. Once Aphrodite had announced her fondness of gods who bathed regularly, all inhabitants of Olympus had scrubbed themselves even when they weren't dirty.

Nick had never before seen the point of bathing when you were clean, but leaning back into the soothing warmth of the tub he understood and then some. This was wonderful. He closed his eyes and smiled appreciatively.

Violet made a soft noise, catching his attention, and Nick opened his eyes to his tub-mate. Hands covering her breasts, Violet watched him, her eyes wide with…fear? No, Nick had seen fear before and she wasn't afraid of him, exactly.

Perhaps she felt like he did, wanted the way he wanted. He reached out a tentative hand to touch her shoulder, this time letting it rest there. The feel of her skin was heavenly. Never had he experienced anything like this. Warm water, warmer woman. Whatever it was she'd put in the water left it feeling silky smooth, with a transparent green tint. The pine smell intoxicated him nearly as much as the scent coming off Violet's skin.

"Nick…" Violet's voice was tentative, unsure. Just the one word spoke volumes.

"It's all right," he told her. "All I want is to touch you."

A funny half-smile covered her lips. "I don't believe you. You want more than that—all men do."

Yes, he wanted more. But he'd take what he could get, what she was willing to give him and nothing more. At the moment she seemed willing to let him do this, so this he would do.

His other hand joined its brother, to grasp her other shoulder, turning her toward him. He ran his fingers along the edge of her arm, to her hand, which hid her breast from his eyes.

He tapped it. "Please, Violet. Can I see what you look like?"

Her eyes turned downcast, shy, but she allowed him to pull her hand away, revealing the tan globe of her breast, tipped in the deepest rose. The nipple tightened under his gaze, and to him it seemed to beckon for his touch.

He obliged at once. The softness of her breast contrasted with the nipple's pebble, soft and hard all at once. He held the mass cupped in his hand, stroked the swollen tip with his thumb, a lovely sensation.

Violet made a soft cry. He took his attention to her face, to see her eyes wide and her mouth open. Again he felt invited—he leaned in to slide his lips across hers, then his tongue went exploring within her mouth, to gently slip across the tip of her tongue. Their second kiss, this one as mind-blowing as the first, in the garden before the rain had come.

So sweet, so erotic at the same time; he pulled back to gaze into her face, trying to fix it in his mind, the look of wonder and dawning passion in her eyes.

So many statues he'd seen—goddesses and nymphs in the gardens and museums he'd occupied since being created. Made from pale marble, they were exquisite creations, features perfect, fair beyond fair.

Here was the reality of Violet, her skin the color of warm earth, its softness that of a new-mown lawn, her pinks and reds all flower hues, her eyes the blue of the sky.

That her nose was short and slightly hooked, that one cheek lifted a little higher than the other, that small spots marred the perfection of her skin—those didn't matter. Cold, perfect marble was nothing compared to this warm, imperfect woman.

She was a garden in herself, alive and inviting, as fertile as the soil of the park. With her there could be growth, seasons, change. Life. A man could spend a lifetime with Violet.

And he had only two nights. For the moment he chafed at the unfairness of it all. Nick wanted Violet not just for one day, but always. He wanted life, not just for now, but the rest of his days. He'd told Aphrodite he'd be content to return to being a statue after being with Violet.

He'd lied.

Violet leaned forward and pressed her lips to his and all thoughts fled from the impact of her kiss, except for one. She would be his tonight and tomorrow. Up to now he'd been a callow youth, and then an object of art, and he'd never known what it was to be a man.

Day after tomorrow he would again be a statue in a garden, but he'd at least know what he was missing. It would have to be enough.

She ran her hand across his chest, lightly caressing his flat nipples, and a shocking sensation spread from that touch, arrowing outwards, then downwards, settling in his groin, in his engorged penis. He hadn't realized nipples were so sensitive, or that touching them could affect other parts of him.

Would it work the same on Violet? She'd certainly made noise when he touched her breast before. He tried it again, and was rewarded by the same sound.

Oh yes, she liked it.

He was about to stroke her again when she moved her mouth to his chest and licked one of his nipples, and the result was like a tiny explosion going off in his mind. When the mental smoke cleared he was gasping for breath and staring into a pair of totally amused blue eyes.

"Like that?"

He managed to answer. "Oh. Yes."

The amusement turned speculative. "You meant that before…about the goddess…and that…" her voice trailed off.

"And that?"

"And that you haven't done anything like this before."

"I was cursed because I refused a nymph who had friends in high places, and died before I ever learned what she'd wanted from me. No, I've never been with a woman. The goddess offered me a special tutor, but I told her I wanted you instead."

Violet's eyebrows leapt for her hairline. "A special tutor?"

Heat invaded his cheeks at her obvious shock. Perhaps he shouldn't have told her. "A nymph, trained in these things. In the experience of love. But I didn't want her." He gazed deeply into her eyes. "I wanted you."

Her gaze dropped away and her hand continued to explore his chest. "No hair. I suppose they didn't model any." Her eyes glanced down. "Not much there either."

Nick licked his lips at her speculative glance. "I was wondering. It feels good when I touch it…"

She blushed. "You were wondering how it would feel if I did the same? Perhaps we should find out."

He could feel his cheeks heat, but embarrassment fled when her fingers laced themselves along the now painfully hard shaft poking out of him.

A mischievous expression filled her eyes and smile. "Don't worry about it, Nick. This is perfectly normal." Another glance down. She laughed. "Well, maybe a bit more than normal."

Normal or not, he'd never felt anything like the play of her hand on him. Slick from the oil-laced water, she stroked him until his mind was aflame and hands clutched the edges of the tub. More, more. Pressure built behind his eyes and deep within his gut.

She continued to touch him, sliding her hand back and forth, teasing the tip that ached every time she backed off.

Oh, yes…like that. And more like that. Again.

Her soft chuckle told him he'd spoken aloud, but he didn't care. She could laugh at him all she wanted, just so long as she kept this up.

Her hand moved like she was milking a goat. Perhaps she was in some sense…such talented fingers. He'd have to compliment her on them later. When he had his senses back.

Then it began, that intense feeling again. It wasn't like anything he'd felt before. Too strong. Too overwhelming.

He was going to die. That was it. Alive for just a few hours, and now she was going to kill him, just with the touch of her hand. A shame, really. But as she stroked him, caressed him, never had he been so willing to give up his life. His stomach clutched, back arched, he moved within her hand, thrusting to keep up the pressure.

Was this pain? No, not pain. Pleasure.

Pulsations began in the organ under her hand and then there was another explosion within his brain, like the one when she'd licked his nipple, but longer and more intense. Long shudders shook him, over and over again, as his organ throbbed under her fingers. He thrust once more and groaned aloud.

Then it was over. He blinked and saw the mischief-laden smile on Violet's face. He gasped and took in a deep pine-scented breath. In the aftermath, deep sensations still rippling through his nerves, his surprise shook him.

He wasn't dead after all.

He looked down, and with a final caress Violet released him, his shaft softening. A milky substance stained the water between them. A hesitant laugh rippled from her as she stared into his astonished face. "Are you okay?"

His confused emotions finally found one to settle on, curiosity. "What did you do?"

Her laugh was nervous. "In the trade, I believe it's called a hand job."

"What I experienced..."

She bit her lip; inwardly he groaned, wanting to bite it himself. Only the idea of getting an answer to his question kept him from dragging her to him and nibbling her lips himself.

"What you did...um...well...you ejaculated." She pointed to the dispersing film. "What you felt is called an orgasm."

It had been so long...he barely remembered his youth, and how his body had worked. He pointed to the water. "I produced that." She nodded. In the fading aftermath of the "orgasm" his mind began to function once more. Memories, facts, things he'd listened to while positioned near the park bench where couples had indulged in various activities. Activities overheard, but not seen.

His finger stirred the water. "This is called semen. It produces babies."

"Under the right circumstances, yes."

His gaze fixed on her. "Will you have my baby?"

Violet's eyes widened and she threw herself out of the tub, water splashing into Nick's eyes, stinging them as he wiped it away.

"I hadn't even thought of that." Worried she gazed at the water. "We'll need protection." She grabbed her heavy robe from the floor and fled the bathroom.

Her sudden departure left him alone, and without her company the cooling water was no longer so nice to sit in. Nick rose and helped himself to a large towel from a nearby rack, using it to remove the water from his body.

As he wrapped himself, he considered her words and actions. She'd initiated what they'd done, the "hand job" as she'd labeled it. He remembered hearing that phrase before and the muffled groans that had followed. Now he knew what the groaning was about.

But her jumping from the tub worried him. She'd acted as if she didn't want any of his fluid on her and he remembered that too, how the female of a couple would say something about protection and not wanting to get pregnant. Violet had mentioned protection—clearly Violet didn't want to have his baby.

He hadn't considered that what he'd wanted to learn might produce a child. Part of him reveled in the idea, that something of him might persist after he was gone, a piece of humanity with his seed in it. Nick imagined Violet, his Violet, a garden bearing his fruit.

But she'd made it clear she didn't want that, and she'd allow him to plant no new life tonight. Despondent again, he leaned against the wall.

He'd been promised love, or at least passion during this time. The goddess hadn't promised more than that, and it was useless to ask for anything else. He wouldn't get it; he was lucky he had this.

From the corner of his eye, he caught a glimpse of his reflection in the clearing bathroom mirrors. He stared at himself, the dark curly hair hanging nearly to his shoulders, the deep brown eyes surrounded by heavy lashes, long straight nose, perfect lips. Perfect lips in a perfect face, he thought bitterly. For a moment he remembered that other day he'd seen his reflection, only to fall madly in love with it.

A foolish young man, falling in love with himself, not realizing the face that haunted him was his own. Now another face obsessed him, Violet's, and he would do anything to be able to view her sweet visage for the rest of eternity.

Chapter Four

In her bedroom, once again dressed in jeans and a sweatshirt, this one decorated with roses instead of daisies, Violet searched the emptiness of Gary's closet for more clothes likely to fit Nick.

There wasn't much left. Gary had been coming into the house while she was gone, out at job interviews or other errands, removing small bits of his existence from her life with every visit. She kept meaning to demand he remove everything so she could ask for his key, but hadn't quite gotten up the nerve to do so.

Besides, as long as some of his belongings remained, it hadn't seemed like he was truly gone for all time. Still, it had become something of a trial over the past week, coming in from a fruitless interview for a job she was over-qualified for, only to find herself searching her home to discover what he'd removed this time.

Today it had been the bentwood rocker they'd purchased together six months ago. When they'd bought it, she'd imagined using it for nursing a newborn baby and rocking her child to sleep in it.

The note he'd left claimed that he'd helped pay for it, so it should go with him. Truth was, he'd paid barely a third of the price, and had never liked it in the first place. He'd only taken it because he'd known how much she loved it. That had been the blow that had driven her to the park this evening, to commiserate with her favorite statue—only to find he'd come to life.

It was true—Nick was really Narcissus, the marble man from the fountain. The look of pure astonishment when she'd touched him in the bath was evidence of that. No way could he have faked that response. For a man to have never known pleasure before—and she'd shown him a pleasure he'd never known, she was sure of that—his explanation, crazy as it sounded, was the only one that made any sense.

She still couldn't quite believe she'd done that. Jerking a man off, and in her own bathtub no less. Put that way, it sounded crude, but it hadn't been. There had been something about the situation, a purity of spirit, so that being sexual with him had been natural. Taking him in her hands had felt almost—religious?

Immediately she backed off from that thought. No religion she'd ever known would have classified the sex act she'd performed as a holy rite. But then, she wasn't dealing with a modern religion. Nick had said Aphredite, or whatever her name was, was the goddess of physical pleasure and had brought him to life to learn about sex. Maybe it was the goddess's influence, making her want to be his teacher.

How did she feel about that? There had been no question about it in the bathtub. A thrill went through her as she remembered the tentative touch of his hand on her breast. What would it have felt like if he'd been certain of his welcome? Suppose those perfect lips had kissed her breasts. Suppose he'd suckled her...a thrill sped through her at that thought.

And the feel of his erection in her hands had been wonderful. He'd been so responsive to her touch and knowing she was giving him pleasure had been empowering. For the first time since Gary left—no, scratch that, for the first time since she could remember—she felt at peace with herself.

Giving Nick pleasure had helped her. Maybe this was what she needed, a couple of nights spent in pleasure with a man who'd be gone in just a few days. No awkward goodbyes, no muss, no fuss.

The perfect one-night stand, because one night…well, two nights would be all they had, all they could ever have. The idea had merit.

Searching the closet, she finally found a pair of faded button-fly Levi's that Gary had gotten too heavy for and a sweatshirt he'd picked up at a sci-fi convention, stuffed in a bag in one corner. On the shirt a leering little green man held up a sign that read, "Mars needs Women. Prefer blonde, 38-24-36, must cook, brains optional. Apply here." Tacky, but it looked warm. Nick might not mind, particularly as he couldn't read English.

Hurrying down the hall with her finds, she encountered her handsome visitor leaving the bathroom. The towel he'd wrapped around his waist did little to hide his appeal and as he spotted her, she could swear the towel bounced a little in front.

Nick was happy to see her in more ways than one.

Suddenly feeling awkward after their close encounter of the sexual kind, she thrust the clothes at him. "Here. Get into these while I make dinner."

"Dinner? You mean food?" An odd light came into his eyes. "I hadn't thought of that. I can eat now." Eagerly he took the bundle. "Can you make—" He named dishes she'd never heard of.

She raised her hand. "Sorry. I don't know how to make anything like that. Tacos are as ethnic as I get, and they aren't from your part of the world. Why don't I do tuna with noodles? That can be pretty exotic."

For an instant disappointment tugged his mouth into a frown and made his eyes sad, but then as quickly as it had been there, it disappeared under his sweet smile. "Whatever you make, I'm sure I'll love it."

Violet suppressed a groan as she watched him traverse the hallway to the bedroom, his perfect backside barely covered by the towel. Gary had never been so cooperative when it came to meals. She had a feeling Nick was going to spoil her for other men.

* * * * *

Heavenly smells came through the door of the room Violet had labeled the kitchen. Dressed in the pants and shirt she'd given him, Nick paused outside, took a deep whiff. Having senses again was a wonderful thing. It had been so long since he could do more than hear or see and even that had been the result of divine intervention. Smell, taste, and touch, especially touch, felt new, it had been so many centuries since he'd experienced them.

This smell he could not recognize. There was something familiar about it, perhaps fish, but otherwise he hadn't a clue as to what it was. He pushed through the door, eager to investigate further.

Violet stood near the cooking surface she'd labeled a stove earlier, flames coming from under a couple of the round black things that dotted the top. She had a round metal object he recognized as a can in her hand, and was scooping bits of white meat from it into a black handled pan, using a forked utensil. A larger pot sat nearby and bubbled merrily over the blue flame beneath it. Violet threw an uneasy glance over her shoulder at him. "I hope this is okay. I've never fed a former statue before. Suppose you can't eat normal food?"

A stool stood nearby. He grabbed it and moved it closer so he could watch her work. "I'm sure it will be fine. Aphrodite knows what's she's doing. She wouldn't turn me human, then leave it so I could only eat gravel."

His joke made Violet laugh, a bright sound that warmed Nick. He'd have to make jokes more often.

At the intoxicating odor coming from the pan, his stomach gave an unfamiliar lurch and made a growling noise, audible above the sounds of the bubbling pot. Surprise filled Violet's face, followed by a sweet grin that left him feeling warm and cozy. "Well, that sounds like a favorable reaction."

She finished stirring the meat into the pot, which he could now see held a thick creamy liquid. Opening a large white cabinet nearby, she grabbed a bag with bright colored pictures of cut vegetables on it, emptying a goodly amount into the pan. As she was returning it to the cabinet, his curiosity got the better of him, and he intercepted it before she could replace it.

The bag was very cold on the outside, frost forming from the humidity in the kitchen. He poured some of the chopped bits of what looked like vegetables into his palm. Orange colored squares, green tubes, yellow kernels, and tiny green ovals filled his hand. They were cold and stiff to the touch. He held out his hand. "What are these?"

"Carrots, green beans, corn, and peas." She took his palm and dumped the contents into the pot. "Frozen, of course. Not as nutritious as fresh, but convenient."

A single yellow kernel clung to his palm. He put it into his mouth and chewed it. His first solid food in three thousand years and it was...he grimaced...not very good. Cold, crunchy, and almost tasteless. He thought of spitting it out but unwilling to make a scene swallowed the offensive item instead.

Violet watched his face, reading his reaction. "Don't worry. They taste better when cooked." That hope buoying him, he watched as she poured pale thin strips from another bag into the boiling water. He reached out and again managed to snatch some from the air. They weren't cold like the vegetables were, but equally hard. Experimentally he tried one, chewing it carefully. At first it crunched, then dissolved into a tasteless paste on his tongue. With great determination, he finished that too.

He let the rest of the strips drop into the water and returned to the stool to mourn quietly. His first meal in three thousand years and it had no flavor or texture to it at all.

Something was very clearly wrong with this world.

Violet's lips were twitching with amusement as she put the rest of the ingredients for their meal away. Opening the cabinet where the cold food was, she pulled out a glass bottle, green in color. "Perhaps you will find this more to your liking." After pulling the stopper with a metal screw, she poured some into a clear glass goblet and handed it to him.

After his previous experiences, Nick sniffed the contents warily. The odor was sharp, with an undertone of sweet, the cold tickling his nose. With an attitude of sheer optimism, he sipped.

Oh, merciful heavens. Wondrous nectar of the Gods—it was wine! Cold as a snow-fed stream, tart as a newly ripe apple, yet sweet at the same time like just-picked grapes. Delicious, delectable, delightful. For a moment he let the golden fluid linger on his tongue until it warmed, and filled his mouth and nose with its essence. Then he swallowed and felt the richness flow to his stomach and a warm glow spread to his fingers and toes.

Speechless, he opened his eyes to see Violet sipping from her own glass. She smiled appreciatively. "Not bad for a cheap Chardonnay, I must admit." Putting her glass down, she returned to the cooking area. "If you'll set the table, dinner will be just a few minutes."

Confusion arose. "Set the table?"

She laughed again. Pointing to some doors over his head, she fed him instructions. "Get the plates from there, silverware is in the drawer underneath."

Eager to please, but unclear what to do, he opened the doors. Thin plates decorated with a pleasing blue pattern were stacked on a shelf. He took two. Opening the drawer, he discovered a plethora of metal pieces, some recognizable like the knife, others he had no idea what to do with. Some were forked like the one she'd used on the meat. Those seemed the most useful, so he grabbed a pair of them, as well as the matching knives.

The kitchen had a table with four chairs set up in the corner. He took his finds there, arranged a fork, knife, and plate next to two of the chairs. He turned to see Violet's approving smile. "You learn fast."

"I try. There is much to learn tonight."

At his oblique reference to their earlier encounter, she blushed, covering her discomfort by sipping more wine.

Nick watched as Violet drained the water from the cooked white strips and put them and the sauce in bowls, which she placed on the table, then took the seat next to him. Spooning some of the strips into the middle of his plate, she covered it with the sauce.

Using his fork to push the food around, he eyed it with apprehension. It certainly smelled better than he'd expected. Next to him, Violet scooped up a forkful of noodles covered with sauce and ate it, obviously relishing the mouthful.

With a resigned sigh, Nick did the same. Astonishment filled him at the subtle taste of the sauce, flavored by the sharp saltiness of the meat, and the blander but still recognizable vegetables. The pale strips were the biggest surprise. Cooked, they were delicious, a wonderful counterpart to the sauce.

When he looked again at Violet, she was quietly laughing. "I guess it tastes better than you expected. Noodles aren't meant to be eaten raw, and the vegetables are more for texture than taste. Not haute cuisine, but not bad either."

"Not bad at all," he managed between mouthfuls. "Best I've eaten in three thousand years." He washed some of it down with the wine and held up his goblet. "And this is wonderful."

"Three thousand years. Has it really been that long?"

"Since I've eaten, yes. When I died, my soul drifted for the longest time, a part of the curse. Then a sculptor was inspired to create my image, and my spirit became tied to that. After that, I've known homes, museums, and gardens." He finished another two bites of dinner, in ecstasy again. "I like the gardens best. The one in your park is my favorite."

Curiosity colored the blue of her eyes, made them brighter. Already attractive, Nick found her enchanting with her questioning look. "Why would you like gardens best? And why our park?"

"I like gardens because they have people in them. A garden is a place to play, to relax. People in museums are sometimes tense. They often don't want to be there. No one is forced to go to a garden." Three more bites disappeared. He began to ration them, put fewer noodles in each bite, so he would have more to savor.

"And the park? Why is ours your favorite?"

He put down the fork and gently took her hand. Staring into her face, he noticed the blush over his blatant caress along her fingers. "I liked your park because it is where I could see you."

Flustered, but clearly pleased, she pulled her hand away. He released it without comment; there would be time later. He picked up his glass to sip more of the ambrosial wine, feeling its heady warmth cushion his mind against the real world around him. He and Violet ate their dinner in a silence of appreciation of good food, good wine, and good company that needed no conversation.

A ringing sound interrupted the peace that had descended. Violet startled at the noise, then even more at the sound of a key in the lock of the front door.

"Excuse me," she murmured, then stood and left the room.

Nick finished the last of his dinner, waited a moment then followed her path to the front room near the door.

Violet stood face-to-face with a man roughly Nick's height, but quite a bit heavier. Sandy brown hair covered his head and chin, and angry black eyes stared out of a face more doughy than anything else.

"What do you mean I should have called first?" he was saying, his voice a low growl.

This must be Gary. Nick had never seen him, but he recognized the man's nasal twang.

Arms folded, Violet's former boyfriend glared down into her face. "Why should I call—it's not like you'd be doing anything. I'm just here to pick up the rest of my things."

He started to move around her, then noticed Nick standing in the doorway. The look of pure shock on his face was something to behold, and Nick felt satisfaction at the man's discomfort.

"What's this guy doing here?" Gary asked with a baleful glance. Another glance took in the sweatshirt. "Hey, he's wearing my shirt!"

Violet's hands fluttered. "His clothes were wet... I didn't think you'd mind."

Gary struck a belligerent pose. "Well I do mind. Tell him to take them off!"

Violet moved between them. "But we got caught in the rain and he hasn't anything else that's dry. I'll wash them and get them to you later."

With a rough gesture, Gary shoved her aside and took two threatening steps toward Nick. Nick held up a placating hand.

"It's all right. He can have his clothes." With one smooth motion he pulled off the sweatshirt, placing it onto the chair behind him. Then he unbuttoned the fly of the jeans, one button at a time, all the time staring at the other man. When he was done, he stepped out of them and laid the jeans on the chair as well.

Gary stared at him, his head bobbing up and down. "You're naked!"

Nick put his hands on his hips and glanced down as well. "Very observant. That happens when clothes are removed, right Violet?" When he looked over at her, she seemed to be suppressing a giggle.

Glaring, Gary turned on her. "What's a naked man doing here?"

It was obviously becoming harder for Violet to suppress her amusement. "Well—he wasn't naked before you made him take off his clothes."

Gary struck a threatening pose. "My clothes," he reminded her.

"Yes, that's right. Your clothes." Nick reentered the conversation. He indicated the pile on the chair. "There they are. You can have them, but you should leave the key in their place."

"What?" Gary spluttered. "I don't have to listen to you!"

Violet broke in. "No, but you do have to listen to me. You can have the clothes, but leave the key. I'm tired of coming home and finding things missing around here."

Gary's piggy eyes narrowed further. "You had it too good when I lived with you. I'll take my stuff and when I'm done I'll send you the key." He moved to grab the clothes off the chair.

With a smooth motion, Nick grabbed his arm and tossed the man over his back, landing him hard on the carpeting. One powerful arm wrapped around Gary's neck in a wrestling chokehold Nick had learned three thousand years ago.

Athenian boys learned to wrestle at a very early age.

Helpless, the other man struggled in vain to free himself, looking astonished at how easy Nick had disabled him. Leaning forward, Nick whispered into his ear. "You are done coming here and disturbing this lady. You can take the clothes, but give us the key." He tightened his hold, and Gary's eyes bugged out. "Don't make me hurt you."

Gary's hand reached out still clutching the key and Violet darted forward to snatch it away. Slowly, Nick released his hold, allowing the man to catch his breath then helping him to his feet. He watched sternly as Gary grabbed the clothes from the chair and backed up out of the house.

On reaching the door, some of his bluster returned. "You haven't heard the last of me, Violet." He glared at Nick. "I'll sue!"

The last of Violet's control was broken and she burst into laughter. She waved the key at him. "Sue who, Gary? The public park?"

Confusion covered the man's face as she slammed and bolted the door behind him.

Chapter Five

Violet's giggles finally wore down and she shook her head at her visitor. "You're naked again."

Nick looked down at himself, not the least bit embarrassed. "That keeps happening." He slid a sly smile at her. "Perhaps it's a sign from the gods."

She snickered at that. "Very funny, Nick. I guess I'll try and find something else for you." Turning, she started for her bedroom, but his hand caught her before she took two steps.

"The clothes you gave me…they were his?"

"Yes…" she answered, uncertain.

Nick folded his arms across his bare chest. "I will wear nothing of his."

Violet exploded. "But I don't have any other clothes that would fit you."

His eyes narrowed and his mouth turned down into a stubborn frown. "It is not important that I wear something tonight. I'm not here to wear clothes and I will have nothing to do with something that belongs to that man."

She paled. "I suppose that goes for me, too."

Nick blinked at her, disbelief in his expression. Then his face darkened in anger. "You think of yourself that way, as that *man's* property?" His emphasis left no doubt as to his opinion of Gary.

He captured her hand and put his other arm around her waist, drawing her to him. "You are your own person, Violet, my perfect woman, a woman deserving of love. I want you to see that. I offered to worship Aphrodite in order to gain the life I needed to prove it to you."

The uncertain feeling she'd had before returned. How could any woman resist this man's warm caring regard? His hands, while they held her firmly to him, were gentle, caressing. He was claiming her as his own.

But only for two nights. That was the problem. How could she make love to a man she'd know for only a short period of time? She didn't doubt his promise that he could teach her that love existed for her—but what of the next day when he returned to his previous existence and left her behind? How would she cope with that?

As she debated with herself, Nick took the initiative again. Bending his head, his lips brushed against hers, much as they had earlier in the park, and again in the bath. Tentative and hesitant, it was not the kiss of an experienced lover, but of one new to the role.

Still, his lips moved against hers in the most beguiling fashion. He may be new to the role, but he was a quick study. His near-innocent kiss left her gasping for more.

She tasted so good. Of their dinner, to be sure, and then there was the sharp tang of the wine they'd drunk. But beneath it all was another flavor, that of woman, of Violet, the sweetest flower of them all.

Surely no other woman ever tasted like this, all sweet and heady, with an earthiness as well. He felt like one of the honeybees that gathered in his garden, dipping into a flower well for its nectar.

If her mouth tasted this good, imagine what the rest of her was like. That thought left him eyeing her clothing, the bulky sweatshirt and jeans she'd donned after their bath. Why would a woman with such lush curves hide them behind these shapeless garments? He vowed to divest her of them as soon as possible—sooner, if he could get her cooperation in the matter. That seemed likely. From the glazed expression in her eyes, she must be feeling some of the same arousal flaming through his veins.

His penis was standing up again and it had been relatively quiet since erupting in the bathtub. What would Violet say to that? Maybe that was one reason for wearing baggy clothes, to hide passionate reactions.

Better distract her before she noticed. He gathered her into his arms and took her to the nearby couch, the soft cushions looking like a fine place to continue their activities. Kneeling, he deposited her, freeing his hands to pull on her sweatshirt, lifting it to seek the warm globes hidden by the thick fabric. Violet gasped when he found them and slid his fingers across the tips of the hardening nipples, repeating the actions he'd noticed she liked so much before.

Soft and firm, smooth and silky. That's what a breast felt like…and here he'd thought them to be hard things, like the ones he'd seen on marble statues. In reality Violet's breasts were like ripe peaches, luscious orbs. Heavy and thin-skinned, they moved under his hand, an exquisite sensation. Violet squirmed as he explored their softness, kneading them gently.

"I want to taste you, I want to know the sweetness of your flesh," he crooned into her ear. He tugged on the edge of the sweatshirt, bringing it up to uncover her fullness. *Oh, so round, so full – they did resemble peaches, very ripe peaches.* He leaned in to taste their tips. So sweet, succulent—the taste of sweetness and cream. Intoxicated by her flavor, he tried each of them in sequence, trying to determine which he liked better, left or right. Did they have the same taste, or not? Was this one more like honey while the other had some lingering tartness?

Violet moaned under his ministrations and he raised his head to gaze at her, noting the rapture in her eyes. "This is pleasure for you, as well?" he asked, breathless.

She wet her lips and he felt a moan of his own rise. "Of course I enjoy it," she told him, her voice throaty with passion. Pulling off the flower-covered sweatshirt, she dropped it on the floor next to the couch. Her shy smile was sensuous as she leaned back.

Naked from the waist up, she was the most beautiful creation he'd ever seen. His hardness ached at the sight, his mouth watering in anticipation. Once again he dipped his head to lick, lave, nibble, and caress her tender globes, enjoying the sweet noises she made as he did.

Eventually her hips began to wiggle on the couch, as if with a mind of their own, and the action drew Nick's attention. He gently stroked the area where her legs met, and was rewarded by her sudden gasp as her crotch rose to meet his hand.

This seemed even more sensitive than her breasts were. Intrigued, he ran his hand under the front of her pants, found the dense forest of curls under her silky undergarment. As he fingered them, her answering groan told him she liked his playing there and he resolved to get her pants off her.

Unlike the jeans she'd given him, these had only one button and a wicked looking metal closure that consisted of teeth and a metal tab. While he continued to caress her breast with one hand, he used the other to ease open the button and then pulled on the tab. It failed to open as he'd expected, so he pulled harder.

Violet's amused chuckle made him realize his actions hadn't gone unnoticed. "Would you like some help with that?"

He gave up control to her, and she lifted the tab up to pull it carefully down the line of metal teeth. As they parted, he could see the silky underwear he'd felt, a light rose color not unlike the tips of her breasts. The comparison dried his mouth and made it hard to breathe.

Underneath the silk were dark curls matted against her skin, the same color as her hair. She pulled off the jeans to drop them on top of her sweatshirt and all that lay between his eyes and the rest of her flesh was that scrap of pink silk..

The urge to tear it off was strong, to shred it, removing the obstacle. But that felt too violent for this encounter. Violet was opening to him, like a flower unfolding from a bud, and that was not a process that went better for hurrying. Instead he touched the delicate fabric, fondled her through it, and felt her answering arousal in the dampening of the silk at the crotch, the pink darkening to a deep rose color.

"You're getting wet."

Her abrupt laugh was breathless and when he glanced at her face her cheeks were as pink as her undergarment. "It's normal, Nick. It's meant to make it easy to slide into me...with your...you know."

Feeling heat rising in her face, Violet broke off. Her role as teacher was hard. She was having a wonderful time at Nick's hands, but his innocent questions kept embarrassing her. Now he smiled at her answer, his brown eyes dark with desire, caring…and something too close to love for her comfort.

She should stop this, put her clothes back on and deny him any further contact. But it felt so good to be wanted by anyone, much less this lovely young man with his gentle hands and loving smile. What harm would it do if they were careful and used protection?

Besides, if she'd understood him right, he'd given up a date with an accomplished seductress to be with her. She owed him something for that.

Violet guided his hands to linger at the edges of her pink-colored underwear. Still holding them, she directed him to pull the panties off, lifting her hips to make the job easier. Kneeling before her, his face turned rapt, alive with eagerness and interest as his gaze took in the skin, hair, and folds now revealed between her legs.

He spread her legs gently, examining this place of feminine mystery for the first time. Thin folds of skin formed lips around a sizable opening into her, surrounded by muscle that clenched at his finger as he gently touched it. The pathway leading to it held more folds of skin, partially obscuring a small nubbin that seemed to throb under his scrutiny. He took his finger and cautiously touched it, and was rewarded with a sharp cry from Violet. Nick glanced up to see her blue eyes wide, her tongue frantically licking those perfect lips of hers.

"Tell me what I'm looking at, sweet Violet. Give me the words."

Her eyes fluttered and she refocused her gaze on him. As her breathing slowed, she pointed to the nubbin he'd discovered. "That's very sensitive. It's called a clitoris, or…just clit." Guiding his hand to the muscle-bound opening, she said, "This is the opening to the vagina. That's where…" Her voice trailed off as he moved his hand into the opening and felt the muscular walls contract again.

Nick eyed the thin flow of fluid building in the entrance and made the connection for himself. "That's where my penis goes," he answered for her. "I understand."

He explored the area with caution and wonder, careful not to hurt her, but too intrigued not to touch the secret places this woman had. It was sensitive, particularly the pearl-like clit, which made her gasp when he touched it, but even touching the soft folds and area around the vagina caused moans of pleasure to build in her.

"Does a woman feel the sort of thing that I felt…" he hesitated, not knowing exactly how to put it. "That is, when you held me in your hand and I…?"

Violet opened her eyes and smiled. "You mean can I have an orgasm? Yes," she laughed. "Although it's been a while…"

"I told you, you have been with the wrong men. I will give you pleasure." Nick spoke firmly, with complete conviction. "Show me what to do."

"Show you?" Confusion crossed her features.

He moved her fingers to where his had been. "You must know how to pleasure yourself. I'm afraid I'll do it wrong without your help. Use your hand to pleasure yourself and show me what to do. Please?"

At his pleading tone and earnest face, some of her shyness faded away. Feeling more than a little self-conscious, she gently fingered the now-hard nubbin of her clit, using the juices leaking below to wet the area. He watched as she did it, saw the nubbin actually grow, and her gasp of breath when it throbbed under her fingers. She moaned and her hips twisted.

It was like watching a blossom bud and flower, the way she reacted, the way she let loose of herself, the way a bud set loose its petals. Her fingers moved in abandon and she reacted in accompaniment, Violet in full bloom.

It was magnificent to see the way she reacted. It made him long to be her fingers, to replace them, to be the one to give her such pleasure. When Nick thought he understood the procedure well enough, he added his fingers into the mix, sliding them over hers, and inserting them into her vagina as well.

Violet's actions changed then…she moaned louder and her hands abandoned her crotch, leaving it to his dominion. She reached for Nick's shoulders, pulling him closer. His mouth hovered over the tip of her breast and without thinking he dived to it, lips clamping onto the nipple, suckling it. Her shudders grew even more intense and she let loose a short scream that communicated her pleasure in no uncertain terms.

When he stared into her eyes, they were so wide with astonishment and passion, Nick couldn't stop the laugh of joy that erupted from him. "I did it, didn't I? I gave you an orgasm, Violet."

Too breathless to answer with words, she nodded. A laugh of her own came out of her, hesitant and thin. "I'm not sure I've ever done that before…quite like that."

He gathered her off the couch and into his arms, held her close to him, resting her in his lap, nuzzling her neck.

Her sweet scent flooded his nose, the flower smell of her hair and skin mixing with the muskier fragrance of her sex, some of which clung to his fingertips. It was a heady mixture, arousing, and his sex throbbed in reaction to it.

Such a powerful feeling, to be able to give pleasure to another. With every touch he'd given her, she'd felt more like his own, that she was his to touch, to taste, to love.

Oh to have that for longer than just these few nights. His mind and body rebelled at the unfairness of it all, that their time together would be so fleeting.

But a bargain was a bargain, particularly when you bargained with a goddess. Day after tomorrow he'd be a statue again, but his soul would have learned what the rest of the world knew.

What it was to love.

Chapter Six

Violet finally recovered her wildly blown senses, to realize she was sitting in Nick's lap, his warm, strong arms cuddling her close to him. His lips brushed her cheek and she felt the warmth of his breath.

"What comes next, sweet Violet? What part of loving do we do now?"

She rested her head on his shoulder, bare under her cheek. Bare? Of course it was bare; all of him was bare, same as her, the pair of them sitting on the floor of her living room without a stitch on.

If Gary could only see her now! He'd always said she was too modest, a total stick in the mud when it came to sex, and here she was stark raving naked in the arms of a man she'd met just that afternoon, a man she'd never see again after tomorrow. Gary would never believe it. She could have never pictured herself like this before this evening.

But then, that was before she'd encountered Nick and agreed to help him learn about love.

Two nights and one day, that's all they had. There wasn't any time to be coy, to be shy; no time to waste.

He was here to learn about sex with her as his teacher, a role she'd never have picked for herself, not in a hundred years. But it was her job and she was going to do it.

She drew herself from his arms and stood, glad she was only a little shaky after the mind-blowing orgasm she'd just experienced. Nick still knelt on the rug, his face wondering. For a moment his pose reminded her of the statue he'd been, although his marble skin was now tan in color.

She reached over to touch his cheek, his beautiful eyes gazing into hers, and her heart melted at the deep affection she saw there. No time to waste at all.

"I think now we'd better move to the bedroom."

His smile was breathtaking as she took his hand, pulled him to his feet, and led him down the hallway.

* * * * *

The bedroom was still disheveled from her clothing hunt earlier, but Nick barely noticed that as they approached the bed. A bed! Big, wide, and probably soft. It might even be bouncy. He pressed down on one edge and watched it spring back.

Nick couldn't resist a happy grin. Excellent. It would make an ideal surface for lovemaking.

He wrapped an arm around her as she pulled the covers back to reveal sheets covered with pale pink flowers. Slipping from his arms, Violet moved to kneel in the center of the bed.

A brief smile crossed Nick's lips as he realized what he was looking at. It was Violet, his Violet, naked and surrounded by roses. Violet among the roses, just as she'd been when he'd watched her earlier this evening. His heart turned over, and he knew for certain that the odd feeling he had whenever he looked at her was more than mere affection, or lust.

What he felt for Violet was love.

He loved Violet, now, tonight, tomorrow, and always. Whenever he thought of her from now on, it would be this image of her he'd imagine, her sweet smile and gloriously lush body, waiting for him on a sheet of flowered fabric.

Waiting for him. She held her hand out and for a moment he hesitated, trying to preserve the image of her for all time, embed it firmly in his heart. Then he could resist no longer. He took her hand and slid onto the bed next to her.

Bending toward her, he captured her lips and they kissed, again and again, her taste once more a revelation to his mouth, the sweet essence that was Violet. Once more he wondered if she tasted the same all over and this time resolved to find out. Pulling away from her lips, Nick trailed kisses down her neck, letting his tongue touch her skin, absorbing her flavor, comparing it as he kissed her from her top of her shoulders, along the ridge of bone there, then down to the beginning of the swell of her breast.

Violet lay back on the bed, letting him crouch above her, giving him leave to touch, kiss, and explore all parts of her in the soft light of the bedside lamp.

He ran his tongue around the outer edge of her softness, encircling it in a narrow spiral until it ended at the peak of her nipple. There he stayed for a moment, feeling the soft bumps and ridges of its pebbled surface.

In the park he'd heard the occasional mother with her infant offspring, nursing it at a nipple much like Violet's. Ruthlessly he killed the image that thought conjured, of Violet nursing his child at her perfect breast.

When it happened, if it happened, it wouldn't be his child. Some other man would plant that seed in her, watch it grow, watch her turn from lover into a mother, and take possessive pride in that transformation.

Some other man would have his Violet as his wife, not him. He was lucky to have her as a lover, even temporarily.

Nick tore himself away from drawing at that single nipple and instead alternated between the two, suckling her nipples until her hips were once more gyrating wildly beneath him and her breath was coming fast. He reached down his hand to the soft mound of curls and it flew upwards into his fingers, telling him how close to orgasm she was again.

But he didn't plan to use his fingers this time. He wanted her taste, *all of her tastes,* to be on his tongue when he again turned to stone.

Nick continued his downward progress, kissing the tender skin at the base of her ribcage, moving across the softness of her stomach, lingering for a moment at her navel, so petite and filled with interesting smells and flavors.

But he had one more place to explore and he got back onto track, trailing a line of kisses to the top of her curls, the same mossy brown as her hair.

And it did look like moss, brown and clinging as on the side of a rock, but this moss covered a much softer substance than stone. When at last his tongue touched the narrow cleft her soft hair hid, the taste nearly drove him out of his mind.

Nectar was never as sweet, and salt not nearly salty enough. She was sweet and salt, tart and mellow, all rolled into one intense sensation, the epitome of all flavors. He let his tongue slide across her clit with one deft motion that left her breathless, then moved her knees up to open her more to him, give him access to all her honeyed parts.

Violet couldn't stifle her groan. She watched as Nick lapped at her folds, his eyes closed, soft moans coming from him along with soft comments about her sweetness. It was all she could do to keep her head with his version of foreplay. She'd come apart once already at his hands, and now he seemed intent on making her do it again, this time with his lips and tongue.

If it hadn't been for his amazing ignorance earlier, she'd never have believed him to be an innocent at oral lovemaking…he was just too good at it! Not the least bit shy, not the littlest bit self-conscious, Nick simply dove in with teeth, lips, and tongue. Especially tongue. He was driving her wild. As she felt another earth-shattering orgasm approaching, Violet gave up fighting it. She ran her hands into Nick's hair, feeling the silky strands slide against her fingers as he continued to work on bringing her to orgasm.

Like a mighty ocean wave, the climax crashed over her, tossed her, turned her, enveloped her in overwhelming sensation, and she screamed his name at its peak. It seemed to go on for hours, immersing her mind in passionate depths, and when at last it was over, leaving her to drift, Nick still continued to lap away at the sweetness between her legs.

Nick had opened his eyes to watch when her muscles clenched underneath him, and added another image of Violet to carry with him. Even the pull on his hair failed to disturb him so intent he was on giving her pleasure.

Finally, as the tremors stilled and her breathing became even, he lifted his head from her still-throbbing mound. Licking his lips to catch the last trace of her nectar, he rose to his knees. His own aroused member stuck straight in front of him, its hardness painful. At once he wanted to know something of what she'd felt.

"Violet," he licked his lips again, watching her face. "My penis is swollen again."

Violet's laugh sounded shaky. "It has many names, Nick. Penis, cock, prick."

"Cock." That was the name of a jaunty rooster, and Nick certainly felt like that tonight. He laughed. "That's a good name. Anyway, I was wondering if you would use your mouth on my cock."

Her eyes widened and she sat up. Mouth in a shy smile, she pushed him onto his back. "I'm not that good at this."

"You'll be fine. I'll let you know what I like. Just follow my lead like I did you."

Violet's beautiful lips closed over the tip of his cock, drawing him into her mouth, and for a moment, he thought he would die of happiness. Moist, wet, hot—her mouth was everything he could have imagined and much more. She sucked and ran her tongue across the narrow opening at the tip, using her hand to stroke him.

Oh, bliss indeed, sweet Goddess, it was bliss to have the mouth of the woman he loved kissing him in this so special way. He'd never again imagine Violet's mouth without seeing it wrapped around his cock.

He felt the urge to push further into her and his hips took up a rocking motion he didn't know they could do. The feeling of before came back, from the bathtub, the sensation of an impending explosion and he nearly let it happen.

Just as it built, a memory impinged, of the many couples he'd overheard in the garden, the number of times a woman would complain of her man "finishing too soon."

He caught Violet's face in mid-stroke, stopping her. Catching his breath, he spoke, his voice harsh in his ears. "I don't know how many times I can do this in a night and I don't want to spend myself just yet."

She pulled him from her mouth and the head of his penis glistened, slick, hard and ready. "I wasn't sure what you wanted—I'm sorry." There was fear in her eyes and voice and for a moment it confused him. Then he realized she was afraid she'd angered him, probably the way some other man had been angry with her.

"No, don't be sorry. Don't ever be sorry with me, Violet. I just want to love you, love all of you the way men and women do." Nick sat up and gathered her into his arms, kissed the worried look off her face and showed how much he wanted her.

There was only one thing left to do, and they both knew it. Apprehensively Violet opened the drawer next to the bed. "I know that you can't make me sick, but I'm not on the pill, and..." Her voice trailed off as her hand emerged from the drawer with a small square package.

Again his experiences in the park helped him know what she held. Protection—she'd spoke of it before, and that's what this was. A condom, if he had the name for it right. Once more his heart sank a little at the thought that no child would result from the love he had for her. He'd leave behind nothing to show he'd been here but a pleasant memory.

But could he really expect anything else? How could he ask Violet to carry his child when she'd have to do it alone? It wouldn't be fair, not to her, not to the child left fatherless. He couldn't be that selfish.

Someday Violet would meet a wonderful man, maybe one who would remind her of him and the love they'd shared tonight. When that happened she could get pregnant and visit him in the park. He'd see her pregnant someday, if not with his own seed, then with that of someone else and it would have to be enough.

He took the package and gave her a reassuring smile. "I know this is needed, Violet. Don't worry so much." He eyed it with some trepidation. "I could use some help though, getting it on."

Her laugh was shaky as she tore open the package and removed the rolled sheath. Placing it on the tip, she carefully rolled it into place, covering him completely.

It felt tight but not unpleasant, and when she stroked him through it he felt wonderful. Then he looked into her eyes and saw the gratitude at his understanding and he felt even better. It was good to be a responsible man, if responsibility resulted in such affection from the woman he loved.

When Nick was ready, Violet lay on her back and directed him to lie on top of her. He fit himself between her legs, felt the opening to her damp with her desire, and fit his condom-clad shaft to it. He pushed forward and felt her stiffen then relax as the tip slipped in. Nick caught his breath at the sensation, the warmth and tightness of her. Gazing into her eyes, he saw the same pleasure as he felt, that she loved the feel of him inside her. Experimentally he pushed further in and her moan almost matched his. Her hips moved and they slid together, centers meeting, his cock embedded deeply within her.

The sensation was fantastic, amazing, like nothing he'd ever known. Even the feel of the condom wasn't a detriment. She contracted around him and he almost lost control.

But he wasn't going to let this end any sooner than he could help. He'd feel his Violet climax again, with him inside her, before he took his pleasure.

Instead he took command and pulled back, then forward again in the simple rhythm that had come so naturally before. Her smile wide, Violet welcomed him, her arms caressing his back, lingering on his buttocks when they drove in again. She kept pace with him and it became as a dance between them, in and out, back and forth, a lover's dance to a music only they could sense, the music of love.

It was the first time for him, the first time for her with him, but it didn't feel that way. Instead it was as if they'd done this before a hundred times or more, so natural, so familiar it seemed. Love was between them, new love, but old love as well. They were lovers now, and lovers are never really new to this dance…it comes too naturally.

Perhaps it was the Goddess' influence that made this so simple. Entwined in Nick's arms, his cock buried deep within her, all Violet could think of was how dear and precious this night was, how much she desired this odd but wonderful man. It barely registered that these few moments were all there would be with him.

Nick knew intimately this was all he would have of Violet, all he could hope to ever have, but could not dwell on that at the moment. How could he when he made love with the woman he desired above all others, and she loved him as well. This was the apex of his life, the culmination of his existence. Two days from now he'd once again be the centerpiece of a garden, but tonight he was Violet's lover.

He whispered loving words into her ears as they moved together, tasted the sweetness of her lips, the softness of her breasts pillowing him as he rocked against her.

It was heaven to be as one with her and he poured his heart out to her in words and gestures, in soft moans of pleasure.

Wonderful, wonderful.

Under him, Violet stiffened, her eyes growing wide and she moved harder with him, driving him to a peak of need he could no longer ignore. With a cry she completed, body pulsing, her hands clenched and face rapt. Her vagina tightened around his cock and he lost control, allowed the spiraled passion to carry him into orgasm.

It was like before, an explosion in his brain, a physical surge in his belly, deep pulsations in his cock that throbbed with his release. The inside of the condom grew hot as it filled and trapped the semen that flooded out of him.

He answered her cry with an inarticulate version of her name and collapsed on top of her, gasping into the pillow beside her.

A prayer formed in his mind. Beautiful, sweet, charming Aphrodite, I will worship at your altar forever.

Chapter Seven

Moving to one side, Nick pulled Violet into his arms, cuddled her close as her breathing began to slow. *So this was love.* He kissed Violet, his emotions twisted and turned, the physical tumult of passion's remains mixing nicely with his wishes, wants, and desires.

One thought stood out—this woman was his. His love, his woman, if only for tonight and tomorrow night.

Twenty-four hours in a day…the goddess had given him thirty-six hours to learn about love.

It sounded like a long time.

It wasn't.

Tonight, tomorrow, tomorrow night. How much of this night did he have left, how much time before dawn? He glanced at the timepiece on the bedside table, recognizing it as a larger form of the small disks people wore on their wrists in the park, but he couldn't read it. What did those squiggles mean? So much he didn't know, even how to tell time.

"What time is it?" he asked.

She glanced at the clock. "Just after eight o'clock."

"And dawn will be?"

"A little after six I think."

Twenty-four hours in a day and he had until dawn the following day. Ten hours left of this night, plus twenty-four, thirty-four hours to spend with her, learn her secrets and hold her close.

Thirty-four hours—not nearly long enough. He nuzzled her neck. "What do lovers do…when they aren't making love?"

He felt her smile. "They talk. About things they have in common, things they want to do. Sometimes things in the past—sometimes the future."

Nick sighed. He had no future with Violet, just a long stint of staring into a pool to look forward to. But even if he could stay, what would he do? He couldn't read, write, or do numbers in this modern time. Illiterate and inexperienced as he was, he wasn't prepared to live in Violet's world.

She seemed to be thinking something similar. "What did you do, Nick, when you were a man?"

"I was the son of a merchant who wished me to become a scholar. I studied in town, learned to read and write. In Greek, of course. I was good at it."

Violet nuzzled in closer to him and rubbed her hand across his chest, toying lazily with his nipples. Tingles started to come from them, and Nick was disappointed when she stopped.

"Perhaps you could become a historian. You probably know a lot about ancient Greece."

Well, that was certainly true. "But there is so much I don't know, Violet. Even if I could stay…"

"You're smart. I bet you could learn."

Could he? Maybe. At least he should learn to tell time, if only so he wouldn't always be asking Violet how much time he had left.

Nick pointed to the clock. "Maybe we could start with something easy. How do you tell time?"

* * * * *

Nick *was* smart. Dressed in her robe, Violet watched as he carefully copied the numbers she'd shown him onto a legal pad, his dark eyebrows furrowed in concentration. Sitting cross-legged on the bed, only a sheet providing modesty, he scowled at one of the numbers on the bright yellow legal pad she'd found for him, and erased it, replacing it with the correct value.

What had started with him learning to count from one to twelve so he could understand a clock, had quickly turned into a full-fledged numbers lesson. Nick had learned mathematics as a child, using Greek acrophonic numbers, a system similar to Roman numerals. After she'd showed him the modern English number equivalents it took him but twenty minutes to master the advantages of a base-ten numbering system.

He chewed the end of the pencil thoughtfully. "This is far more efficient. I can write very large numbers using fewer symbols." He wrote down the number 9999. "It would take me thirty-six symbols to do this." He eyed the pencil. "And this is much less cumbersome than a stylus to use."

Nick raised a hopeful eyebrow. "Do you suppose you could show me how to read some of your symbols for words?" he asked eagerly.

She laughed. "Maybe later. You're going to be here tomorrow."

A hungry look came into his eyes that Violet recognized. Immediately her center responded with a flood of desire. “Well, then…what else can we do?” he asked in a husky voice.

A bell rang from the distant living room, startling them both. Violet’s eyes widened and she stared at the clock, just as the bell rang again. She jumped from the bed, her face showing a dawning horror.

“Oh, no, I forgot! It’s group night!”

“Group night?” Nick stared in confusion as Violet hopped about the room, grabbing yet another sweatshirt adorned with painted flowers, this time daffodils, and another pair of her apparently unending supply of baggy jeans.

She struggled with one of her shoes while answering him. “Group night. I forgot, it’s group night, and I’m hosting. I’m in this group, for women…” She got the one shoe on and looked under the bed for the second. “…women who’ve had trouble with men. We meet on Thursday evenings at nine o’clock for dessert and…” Obviously spying it, she disappeared beneath the mattress, her voice muffled. “…talk.”

“Talk?” Nick wrapped the sheet around him, trying to make sense of Violet’s turbulent running around.

“Yes, talk.” Dressed, Violet paused in the doorway. “Talk about what bastards men are.” A third time the bell rang, this time far more insistent, the buzzer going a long time before easing off. Violet threw a desperate glance at Nick. “I can’t explain you. Just stay here and be quiet while I’m gone. It’ll only be an hour or so.”

* * * * *

“Well, good riddance, Abbey, that’s what I say.” Marge leaned back and took another sip of her decaf coffee, condemnation and scorn decorating her face. "There isn't a man alive that's worth our tears."

Violet watched as Ali and Helen nodded in agreement with their outspoken friend. Both were two years divorced, same as Marge. She and Abbey were the only ones who'd never been married, but like the other three, their relationships with men had rarely been anything but disastrous in the long run.

Gary at least had lived with her for a while. Abbey's boyfriend wanted to move in, but the military kept him hopping from one location to another.

"Oh, I don't know," Abbey said softly, her gentle expression showing her dismay. "It wasn't like Howard wanted to leave me. But when the army says you need to go, you need to go."

Marge helped herself to another brownie from the plate and spoke around the mouthful. "If he'd really loved you, he wouldn't have left, even if he'd had to desert."

"But they put people in jail for that. Besides, Howard has too much honor to desert his post. What do you think, Violet?" Abbey appealed. "You don't think he should have gone to jail for me."

"No, of course not." Sometimes Marge went too far, this definitely being one of those times. No way a man should go to jail for his ladylove - any more than he should return to being a statue, she realized, comparing her problem to Abbey's. Both of them had men who wanted to stay, only to be ordered elsewhere.

Why couldn't Nick stay here with her? What would happen if he didn't return to the park? Maybe if he didn't, Aphrodiddy, or whatever her name was wouldn't be able to turn him back into a statue.

Surely by now Nick had served his punishment for self-absorption, even in the minds of gods who must have memories as long as their lives. Nick certainly wasn't a man who only thought of himself now. When he made love to her, it was her pleasure he sought first, not his own.

Nick was the most unselfish man she'd ever been in bed with. If only there was something she could do for him.

Violet settled back on the couch, trying to ignore the lump under the cushions from the clothes she'd stuck there before answering the door. She'd spent a scant few moments to clean the place up after leaving the bedroom, grabbing her clothes from the floor next to the couch and hiding them.

Fortunately, jeans and sweatshirts didn't wrinkle badly, but they did add bulk to the cushion underneath her. Sipping her own decaf coffee, she tried to stay focused on the conversation around her rather than wondering what Nick was up to in her bedroom.

"Well, at least Violet's doing all right," Marge's deep voice boomed approvingly. "I would have expected to find you in a puddle of tears after that jerk dumped you."

She had been…but that was before Nick. Not that she could tell them that…

"Who is THAT?" Ali's mouth dropped open from her spot on the chair facing the hallway. Turning, Violet spied her green robe clinging to a much larger frame, disappearing from the hallway into the bathroom. After a while, a thin trickling sound came through the open doorway.

Three thousand years as a statue must not have interfered with his needing the toilet. Of course, she remembered, they'd drunk a fair amount of wine. For a moment she wondered if he'd understand how to use the facility, then the sound of flushing answered the question. She smiled—very clever these ancient Greeks.

Then she turned to face her audience and heat permeated her cheeks under the steady stares of her friends.

"Why, Violet. Were you entertaining?" Marge asked in a dangerously sweet voice.

"No wonder she's not upset over Gary." Helen added.

Violet fought the urge to tell them to go to Hades and kick them all out of the house. "Nick is an old friend of mine," she said. Well, that was true enough. Three thousand years certainly counted as old, and she'd known him most of her life… sort of. "He's staying with me."

"Oh really? Staying in your bedroom?" Ali questioned, her eyes dancing with dangerous humor.

The splashing sounds from the bathroom ended and Nick reappeared. He was moving surreptitiously down the hall, as if trying not to be noticed.

Ali called after him. "Hey, Nick! Come in here and introduce yourself!"

Freezing in place, he turned slowly, cautiously, as if debating what to do. Then, resignation screaming from his posture, he approached the living room, apprehension written all over his handsome face. His approach made Violet think of a Christian facing the lions in a Roman coliseum. On entry to the room, his gaze darted between their faces. When it landed on Violet, quiet regret was in his eyes.

"I couldn't wait to go any longer," he whispered. She tried to convey her understanding with a quick shrug and a smile, and some of the concern in his face melted away.

Then Marge spoke. "So, you've known Violet long?"

"Most of her life," he answered, wariness returning to his stance.

"Where did you meet?"

"In the park. When Violet was a child." He smiled at her, and even with the stress of the moment Violet found herself melting under his warm regard. "She was a beautiful child."

The cross-examination continued. "Oh? You live near here? How come we haven't seen you before?"

"I don't exactly live here..." Nick began.

Fearing an explanation that would raise more questions than answers and involve unusual deities, Violet jumped into the fray. "Nick's only here for a short time. Just a couple of nights, actually. On business."

Helen snickered and eyed the robe, which barely fit across Nick's chest. "Business? What's he doing in your robe?"

"My clothes got wet in the rain," Nick told her.

"And the airline lost his luggage," Violet improvised wildly. "Nick's looking into a position at the university in the ancient studies department and is only here overnight."

"And he's really just a good friend," Marge finished with an amused air. "So, good friend Nick, what did you think of Gary?"

A scowl twisted Nick's handsome face. "The man is pond scum," he said flatly. "Completely unworthy of Violet's affections."

All four other women burst into laughter and applause, while Violet squirmed under their amusement. Nick didn't have to be quite so blunt.

"We've been telling her that for months," Helen got out between guffaws.

"No man is worthy of a woman's affections," Marge noted scornfully. "That's what I always say. None of them can be trusted further than they can be tossed."

"I don't believe that's true," Nick said. "There are many men deserving a woman's love. I've seen it time and time again, people in love. Not every man is like Gary. Most aren't like him... but you have to know what to look for, what makes a man a good lover."

Marge eyed Nick like a cat would a mouse...just before pouncing. "Okay, expert. What makes a man a good lover?"

"Caring, for one thing. Caring for more than just himself. It doesn't even have to be that a man cares for a particular woman. The man who picks up loose paper in the park so it doesn't foul the duck pond, or the one who makes sure his dog doesn't leave a mess on the pathway—these men are worthy of love, because they take care of the world."

"So, you're suggesting we hang out in the park and look for losers who pick up after their dogs?" As usual, Marge's voice had gone beyond skeptical into pure scorn and Violet cringed at her friend's ill temper being turned on an innocent like Nick. He didn't deserve Marge making fun of him.

But she couldn't really blame Marge, either. She knew the source of the woman's pain. Her husband of seven years had left her when she'd undergone surgery for breast cancer, telling her he'd hadn't signed on to live with a woman who wasn't whole anymore. The fact that her Harry had become half again the size he'd been when they'd married, with a beer gut and thinning hair to boot, didn't seemed to strike him as important. He could have done something about his belly, at least. Certainly Marge would never have divorced him over it.

But Marge being one breast less made her too flawed for him, so abandon her he had. Now that was a man who was pond-scum.

Nick's thoughtful smile suggested he hadn't understood Marge's sarcasm and had taken her question as serious. "There are worse places to meet someone. A lot of nice people go to the park."

He thought for a moment. "For example, I know one man who brings his little girl to the park every afternoon to play. He loves her very much but taking care of her in the afternoon and evenings doesn't give him many opportunities to meet nice women. If one of you were to go there, maybe with a book to read, perhaps you could find him."

Helen perked up and Violet remembered how she loved children but had been unable to have any of her own. "A little girl? How old?"

Nick shook his head. "I'm not very good with ages, but they've been coming there for a few years. I guess she must be six or so."

"A six-year-old girl..." Helen's face grew wistful as her voice trailed off.

"Then there is a big man who has a booming voice. He comes and sits on the bench in the rose garden on Saturday afternoons. He feeds the ducks and I've heard him talking to them. He's very lonely since his wife died, they used to feed them together." Nick glanced over at Marge thoughtfully. "His wife was something like you."

Now Marge's eyes held a thoughtful expression, but suspicion crossed Ali's thin face. "How is it you know so much about the people who hang out in the park when you're from out of town?"

"I've spent far more time in the park than anywhere else when I've been here. It's a lovely place."

Abbey laughed. "No wonder you've got so much in common with Violet. The park has always been her favorite place. When we were girls she'd always want to spend the afternoon there. I didn't mind though, I loved it too. Beautiful trees and lawns, and the gardens are lovely."

"Me, I like that statue they have there," Ali added. "The marble one of the man staring into the pool. He's a real hunk, if you ask me. Too bad they had to put clothes on him."

"A real hunk?" Nick laughed. "You think so?"

"Sure, ask anyone...that guy is yummy. I wish I could meet the model for it," she said with a grin.

A surge of unreasonable jealousy sped through Violet. Not that she cared that Ali liked staring at the mostly naked Nick when he was a statue. It was the way her friend stared at the non-marble Nick that burned her up.

Ali nudged Violet gently with her elbow, a mischievous grin on her face. "You've always had a little thing for him, too, haven't you, Violet? I've seen you spending lots of quality time with that statue in the park."

Violet resisted the temptation to elbow her friend back, much harder. "I've always loved spending time in the park, Ali. And it wasn't the statue's body I was staring at."

Chapter Eight

Nick listened to them banter, leaning against the edge of the couch, his fingers resting on the cushion behind Violet's head. The urge to run his hand down the back of her neck and feel her smooth skin was overwhelming, but he didn't dare do anything of the sort at this point, not with her friends there.

He shouldn't even be in the room with them. Violet had made it clear he was supposed to stay hidden until they were gone, but when nature called, it called. After so many centuries of not having bodily functions, he'd been surprised at how fast his new form adjusted to being alive. Nick had hoped to sneak down the hall and make it back before he'd been noticed... but, of course, they'd noticed him.

Now he'd embarrassed Violet, who obviously didn't want her friends to know they were lovers... if only temporarily.

A dismal thought occurred to him. Maybe she only wanted him for the time they had and even if he could stay longer, she wouldn't want him anymore. He gazed at her beautiful profile in melancholy appreciation.

It didn't matter if she didn't want him for longer—he couldn't stay anyway. Aphrodite would never agree to let him stay for more than the time he'd been given. She couldn't, not without risking the anger of the gods who'd sentenced him in the first place. While the goddess might risk a reprimand or two in the pursuit of her own amusements, she'd never go against the others.

The women were still discussing the merits of men he'd mentioned, the lonely ones from the park. Perhaps they would take his advice and go there, look for the men who deserved love. Maybe his being here could change their futures. There was some hope in that and he should feel good about it.

But he didn't. He was one lonely man who didn't have a future and who would never deserve love.

Nick cleared his throat and caught their attention, the strangely beautiful faces of Violet's friends turning toward him. So different from the faces of stone he was used to...imperfect, flawed, yet gloriously lovely in their humanity. Their smiles warmed him in a way he'd rarely known before.

Only Violet's smile set him on fire. He glanced down at her and felt the now familiar raging in his blood and loins, and was grateful for the covering bagginess of the robe.

"It was nice meeting you, but I should leave you alone and let you get on with your meeting," he said and rose to leave the room.

As one, the other four women leapt to their feet. "Oh, we'd better be going, ourselves," Marge said, with a side-glance at Violet. "It would be rude for Violet to ignore you when you're only going to be here a short time."

"Oh, yes...very rude," Ali added, grinning. "We'll just show ourselves out."

While the four grabbed their coats and hastened to take empty cups to the kitchen, Violet put up a mild protest that everyone ignored. Soon the group was moving through the door, hugging and kissing cheeks and promising to catch up next week, this time at Helen's house.

It was Ali who had the final comment on his presence. "Lovely meeting you, Nick, and I'll see you around the park!" she chirped as she pulled her car keys from her pocket.

He smiled at her, hiding the sadness he felt. "I'm sure you will."

She flashed him a grin and disappeared through the door and finally Nick and Violet were alone again.

"Are you angry with me?"

Violet turned to see Nick's brown eyes dark with concern, uncertainty in his face. "Why would I be angry, Nick? You haven't done anything wrong."

"I just thought…you were bothered that I was here when your friends were."

"It was awkward at first. I was afraid—well, never mind what I was afraid of." Nick was from a different time and place and conversed with the goddess of physical love. How could she explain to him that intimacy as instant as theirs, the proverbial "one-night stand", was normally forbidden to "nice girls" and that in spite of allowing Nick, practically a stranger, to stay with her tonight and make love to her, she was still a nice girl.

She'd been afraid her friends would guess the truth about their relationship, make the logical jump to conclusions, particularly since he wouldn't be there after tonight.

But then she'd realized that if her friends judged her that way, they wouldn't really be her friends. She laughed at the memory of their faces. "It was funny when you began matchmaking for them. Do those men really exist?"

"Of course they do. I wouldn't make them up." Nick almost looked offended. "I couldn't describe them because I've never been able to see them. Only yesterday was I able to see more than my own face in the fountain. But I've heard them speak, I've listened to them."

"It'd be funny to see if they go to the park and find out for themselves. I notice you didn't suggest a man for me," she teased.

Pain crossed his features. "I…I don't like thinking of you with someone else. I should though." He shook his head, frustration ebbing from him. "I have so little to offer you."

His sweet concern touched her and she threw her arms around his waist, burying her head in his chest. Breathing deeply, she filled her lungs with his warm smell, of man and sweat, the result of their earlier lovemaking. "You offer me love, Nick. What more can any woman ask for?"

He crushed her to him, the strength in his arms a surprise. "I would give you anything, Violet, if it would mean you'd stay with me. I would give anything to be with you. You say I give you love, but even that is only temporary, for a short time…too short."

"I'll take what I'm given and appreciate it—a night, two, or a lifetime." His pain became hers, their dilemma cutting deep into her soul. "If this is all we have, then let's make the most of it."

She lifted her face to his, and he captured her mouth, drawing her into a long, lingering kiss. Lips slid against lips and tongues intertwined and once more Violet was overwhelmed by Nick's flavor. She reveled in it, let her hands play across his back, the taut muscles under the robe.

Leaning back, he had a peculiar expression on his face. "Your taste has changed." Running his tongue over his lips, his eyes widened with appreciation. "What is that?"

For a moment she wasn't sure what it was either. Then realization hit and she pointed to the plate of brownies on the table. "We were having coffee and dessert."

"Coffee? Dessert?" Excitement took over Nick's face. Then he seemed to remember his manners. "Could I have some?"

Violet burst into laughter at his hopeful tone. "Of course, just a minute and I'll get you a cup."

When she returned from the kitchen, a fresh cup in hand, Nick already had one of the brown squares in his hand and was eyeing it suspiciously. "It certainly smells good," he told her, a dubious tone in his voice.

Amused anticipation bubbling through her, Violet poured some decaffeinated brew into his cup and placed it before him. "Why don't you take a little bite and see if you like it."

He did, just the tiniest nibble and his eyebrows shot clear to his hairline. "Oh praise the gods, that's wonderful! What is it?"

"Chocolate, Nick. That's a chocolate brownie, a kind of rich cake. To most of us chocolate is the food of the gods. Go ahead, take a bigger bite."

He did, and the resulting moan of ecstasy made her glad that her friends had left. They might have believed many things, but no one could have missed knowing this had to be Nick's first experience with chocolate. He rolled his eyes, his bliss evident even in the way his jaw moved, slowly, then slower, letting the flavor stay in his mouth longer, waiting until the last moment to swallow.

He groaned, and for an instant Violet wondered if he was going to have another orgasm. She handed him the cup of coffee, and he took it, and sipped the brew carefully.

Again he groaned. "That was good too. Not as good as the brownie, but the combination is wonderful."

She indicated the still half-full plate. "Well, enjoy yourself. I guess you don't have to worry about having a weight problem."

Sipping a fresh cup of decaf, Violet watched Nick consume the rich dessert like there was no tomorrow. For him, there really wasn't, or at least not more than one. He ate two more brownies before he seemed to realize she wasn't eating any.

Looking guiltily at the third square in his hand, he offered it to her. "Don't you want one?" he asked.

She shook her head reluctantly. "No, I can't. I have to watch my weight, I'm too fat already."

He stared at her, consternation in his expression. "What are you talking about, Violet? You aren't the least bit fat."

"I am." She pinched her waist, taking in a good inch of skin. "See?"

Nick exploded. "That's skin, Violet. It's supposed to do that. It's thick there, that's all."

"But I'm not thin, like…" She stopped when she saw him shaking his head gravely.

"There is nothing wrong with your shape, Violet. Yours is a womanly figure, that of someone who enjoys life. You don't ritually starve yourself, or deny your appetites…except for maybe one." He moved closer and she again saw hunger in his eyes, a hunger that had nothing to do with the brownie in his hand. He put it aside before he took her into his arms.

He'd promised to show her love, to prepare her for another man, but deep inside she knew that was a lie. Nick could no more give her to another man than she could give him to another woman.

They were made for each other. What a shame they couldn't stay together.

"Nick, I want you now. Take me to bed."

He didn't need another invitation. In moments they were in the bed, entwined as before, and this time when he entered her it was even more intense, quicker, the result of desire too intense to ignore. They were no longer strangers making love, but lovers repeating something precious to the pair of them.

Love made, given, and taken. Love in the physical…but moving on. Moving to something more, more precious than sex.

Love-making migrating to love-giving.

Nick pulled Violet's arms higher, holding them against the pillow and stared into her face, flushed with exertion. Her beautiful face, eyes bright with affection and desire for him.

For him!

His lover, Violet, in his arms, under his body, her arms aligned with his, her core clenching his cock as he drove into her. His Violet. His. Lover, woman, his.

His!

She was his. No other man should hold her like this, possess her like this.

His lips descended on hers, wanting to brand her, to show her she belonged to him. She accepted his kiss and returned it with equal fervor. Perhaps they were branding each other.

Nick moved again within her and she responded, her cries growing more intense with each move he made. Possessiveness took a new hold on him and his hands bound her wrists like manacles, tying her to the bed as his pace picked up. She didn't fight him, but moaned a little as his grip tightened.

Through his passion, Nick heard her. He checked his driving pace. "Am I hurting you?"

Her eyes were wide and her breathing quick. "A little."

Shame temporarily replaced his ardor and he released her, using his arms to brace himself off her. Staring down into her loving face, Nick once again vowed to himself that he'd never cause harm to her.

He tried a crooked smile. "I'm sorry, Violet. I guess you bring out the beast in me. I can't help wanting to make you mine."

Her hips moved under him, reminding him just how much of her he already owned. "You and I are already part of one another. You don't need to hold me onto the bed. Unless you're really worried I'm going to escape you!"

Grinning, Nick used his cock to possess her instead of his hands, and to his pleasure Violet responded. The moans she made this time were pure ecstasy and he found them far more intoxicating. Moments later Nick climaxed, dimly aware that Violet had followed him into that blissful state, her throbbing core gripping him as she came.

He collapsed on top of her, breathing into her neck for a long time. When he was able to form a coherent thought, he leaned up to gaze into her face. "You were right. I don't need to bind you."

Violet turned pink and chuckled. "Bondage is a little more advanced than we need to get into here."

He didn't quite understand her, but accepted her word on the subject. Sliding off her, Nick pulled the covers over them, Violet finding a place to rest her head on his shoulder. She relaxed into his still-aware body. "What do lovers do, Violet, when they aren't making love? Or talking?" he asked.

Violet giggled then glanced at the clock. "What time is it, Nick?"

He checked and returned to gaze at her sheepishly. "It's nearly twelve. I guess it is getting late."

She smothered a yawn. "I love having you here, but I need to sleep, Nick. I have another job interview tomorrow and I want to be rested for it."

Nick pulled her closer. "Then I guess what lovers like us do is sleep together."

Resting her head on his shoulder she found herself cuddled close, the hardness of his thighs trapping hers.

His penis stirred but he kept it a secret. One hand idly caressed her back and he kissed her forehead. "Good night, Violet. Sweet dreams."

No longer able to suppress her yawns, Violet gave in and tumbled into sleep. "Good night, Nick," she muttered. "I'm glad you're here."

"So am I, Violet. So am I."

*****

For a while he let his mind follow one line of thought after another, hoping the chase would exhaust it and let him slumber. To be able to sleep, to dream, truly dream for the first time in centuries—it sounded like heaven.

But sleep eluded him like a shy nymph did a randy satyr, and when he watched the clock numbers tick the hour over for the second time, he finally gave up the race.

After so much time as a statue, he simply wasn't tired enough to sleep. Perhaps later he'd find some rest.

Violet only stirred a little as he pulled from her arms and allowed her to roll over to rest her head on her pillow instead of his chest. Her mouth fell open and a soft sigh came from her. His body reacted as it always did, to full readiness. His shaft might as well be still made of stone it was that hard.

This was going to be a long night. He couldn't wake her and make love to her again. She needed sleep for her job interview. If he stayed here, her softness would drive him crazy with want.

Maybe he'd better find another place to spend his sleepless hours.

Her robe lay on the floor, and he put it on. It fit, not comfortably, but sufficient. Moving to the door, he eased it open, careful to not disturb the bed's slumbering occupant.

In the living room, he turned on just one of the table lamps and settled into the big armchair he'd admired before. Almost a throne in size, its softness felt wonderful.

One thing about kneeling in place for centuries, it gave you a real appreciation for being able to sit on your rear.

A pile of books lay on the table, the covers bright and illustrative. On one a man rode a massive horse, a woman sideways behind him. The horse was magnificent. With hope of more pictures he opened it up and was disappointed to find nothing but words inside.

If only he could learn to read. What wonders must exist in these books, tales of people great and small? In the park there were often people with books in their hands, resting on the benches and enjoying nature and a good story at the same time.

He looked at the clock on the wall, a circular one with the numbers along the side and large hands that indicated the time, instead of what Violet had called a "digital" clock in the bedroom. The big hand was on the six and the small one partway between the two and the three. Violet had told him to multiply five times every number, so five times six was thirty.

Or…the hour was halfway between two and three…also two-thirty! Satisfied with his accomplishment, Nick looked about for something else to conquer. After picking up a couple more books on the little table, he replaced them reluctantly.

They would have to wait until he could learn his letters as well as his numbers. A small box next to the books caught his eye. It was oblong, black, with small buttons labeled with numbers, zero and one to nine. There were a few words, but not many.

Curious, Nick picked it up. Pushing the buttons didn't seem to do anything and he was just about to put it down when he tried the large red button at the top. Immediately the window on a large box in the corner of the room sprang to life, the glass lighting up from within and images forming across it, sound coming from a hidden source.

Nick gaped at the sight. What a marvel! He pushed a button with a little arrow on it that pointed up. The sound increased and he panicked. He didn't want to wake Violet. He tried the button next to it that pointed down, and the sound decreased.

He breathed a heavy sigh of relief when nothing stirred in the bedroom. He'd have to be more careful!

Behind the glass screen he saw a group of men wearing big hats threatening in a slow drawl to go after some varmints. They had horses with them, really nice ones moving restlessly in the background.

He moved up to the box and reached out to touch the glass, wishing he could get closer to the animals. He'd always loved horses.

The men swung up onto the animals' backs and rode across the open desert around them. Nick was fascinated at how the box kept up with them, that the men on horseback were always at the center of the screen. Then the scene changed and he was looking at another man, this time all in black, crouched at the top of a hill. He aimed a long tube, which jerked and smoke came from the end. The scene changed again, back to the men on horses, and one of the riders cried out and fell off his horse.

Nick gaped as the riders all stopped and jumped off the animals, taking off for the surrounding bushes and rocks. They aimed their own small metal tubes up the hill, and smoke poured out the ends.

He realized he was watching a battle between the men and the man in black, who was undoubtedly the varmint they'd ridden after. The weapons were likely guns. He'd heard similar sounds late one night in the park, when the authorities of the law had come to capture some people exchanging money and small bags. He hadn't seen them anymore after that night.

But these men were dressed in clothing unlike those worn now, and the way they spoke sounded like a play of some sort.

Perhaps it was? Another man clutched his chest and his eyes squeezed shut as if he was in pain. He collapsed against the boulder, but Nick noticed no blood on his shirt when his hand fell away.

One of the people shot in the park had fallen into his fountain, and the blood had stained the water and surrounding marble for days until the park authorities had scrubbed it clean. He still remembered the wounded man's gasps and cries and how long they had lasted, even after others had come and pulled him off the fountain and onto a stretcher.

The man in the box had died too fast and bled too little. This wasn't real life on the box. It must be some sort of entertainment like he'd heard sometimes from his pedestal, something like "Shakespeare in the Park." It must be a play!

Reassured he wasn't watching the slaughter of real people, Nick settled back into the throne-like chair to enjoy the show. For a while there was more talk and horse riding, then abruptly the screen changed to something completely different, the sound jumping at the same time. Desperately Nick stabbed at the down-arrow button on the box in his hand.

This new show had people talking directly to him, as if they could see him. Maybe they could and if so…Nick tugged Violet's robe closer around him. No point in taking any chances that they really could see his cock hanging out. But if the people on the show could see him, they gave no sign of it, and Nick relaxed. He must be wrong…the big box was a one-way delivery system of images and sound. That was all.

The new show ended, and another one began, just as loud and again with no obvious connection to the men on horses. This time the subject seemed to involve whiter teeth.

As if his teeth needed to be any whiter—they were still the same color as the marble he'd been made from. Frustrated, Nick picked up the little black box and tried one of the other buttons with an arrow. The screen changed, and now there were men dressed as law officers running down an alley after a poorly dressed man with fast feet, who turned and fired another of those short tubes at them. This man's weapon was smaller and sleeker than those of the men with the big hats. He shot, they shot, he shot, they shot, and then he ducked behind a wall and ran away. The police couldn't find him so they walked back to their shiny black car and drove away.

Nick couldn't make sense of this show at all. If the men shot so many times, why didn't they hit each other? Were they that bad at it? And why give up? He tried hitting the button again and a new program appeared.

Nick's eyes widened in appreciation. *Now this was more like it!* Men and women dressed in Grecian garments stood around a marble temple, their speech stilted and formal as they addressed each other. He even thought he recognized a name or two…Oh…they were praying to the gods, Eros and Aphrodite.

Enthralled, Nick settled deeper into the big armchair as the men and women moved into the temple, pairing up when going through the porticos into the main hall. As they passed inside, he noticed them moving off to take positions by the furniture of the room, the narrow divans and chairs, arms entwining.

The screen focused on one couple, who embraced and kissed, a deep, open-mouth kiss. Nick admired the technique, the strength in the man's arms as he held his lady to him. Masterful! Possessive. The man controlled their clinch, but there was no force to it. Instead the woman leaned into him, her eyes bright.

The man thrust the woman back and pulled her dress from her shoulders, the gown giving with a ripping sound and falling away, revealing her body in its natural glory. Nick's eyes widened at the woman's heavy breasts tipped with erect nipples, and the neatly trimmed hair surrounding the entrance to her woman's parts. She must cut it, to make it as even as that. He imagined Violet's soft mound like that, and decided it might look pretty good.

The sudden unclothing of the woman didn't seem to faze her. Breasts bouncing, she reached over to tug at the man's tunic, and it fell away, revealing wide shoulders and a powerfully built torso covered in a significant amount of hair, across his chest and particularly at his crotch. Sticking out of the middle of the lower bush was an erect penis the size of a log.

A small log, but still…Nick gaped at the man's size. Good thing Violet was asleep. She was pleased with him, but obviously she'd had little experience with other men.

If she saw this she might have something to compare him with.

The couple faced each other and the man seized the woman's arms, dragging her closer. In the background Nick saw other couples baring their bodies, and the significance of the salute to Eros and Aphrodite took on new meaning. The people in this show were going to have sex, lots of sex, from the looks of things!

Maybe he could learn something! Nick leaned forward.

The man's head dipped to capture one nipple, his hand fingering the second. Head rolling back, his lady moaned delicately, then more earnestly as her partner moved one hand to the juncture of her legs and delved deeply. Lifting her, the bulky man balanced her slender body with her legs across his shoulders, opening her pussy to allow his mouth to play where his fingers had already been. A sharp cry came from her as his mouth descended.

What strength this man had! Nick doubted he could lift Violet so effortlessly, nor hold her in place once she was there. He flexed his arm muscle. There wouldn't be much time for building up his body before he returned to stone.

Maybe he could learn something else, something easier to accomplish. Returning his attention to the screen, he discovered that the couple had changed position, and the woman was now using her mouth to pleasure the man, tongue slipping along the length of his cock to lave the head with long licks. A shot of the man's face revealed his enjoyment of that activity. Nick smiled in memory of how Violet had done the same to him.

The scene changed and moved around the room, revealing couples similarly engaged in various kinds of foreplay. Some positions and activities were new to Nick and he noted the ones that looked the most appealing.

Did a woman really enjoy having a man's thumb in her ass? He wondered at that, and decided he'd ask Violet about it later…maybe much later.

Foreplay had ended in some cases, and couples were actively engaged in intercourse. One woman was on her hands and knees, her partner entering her from behind, pumping madly away. In that position, he was able to lean forward and fondle her breasts, tweaking the nipples as she gasped her delight. When his other hand reached for and apparently found her clit, the woman lowered her head and gave a deep moan. She drove back into his cock, taking his rhythm and increasing it, her pendulous breasts keeping time with her movements. Their sway was almost hypnotic.

Now that was something he could aspire to. Imagining Violet's breasts in place of the unknown woman's, and her magnificent ass in front of him, him buried deep within her…Nick's cock stiffened under the robe.

The scene changed again and this time Nick watched as two men stood and held a woman aloft, face down. She suckled one cock while the other man penetrated her from behind. All three seemed intent on their activities, low moans and groans coming from them.

Nick considered that. No, not for him…he wasn't interested in sharing Violet's body with another man. Similarly he rejected another trio, even though here the two women were playing with each other's breasts as the man slid his cock into one of them.

He'd met Violet's friends and doubted if any of them would be interested in that kind of game.

Other small groups were forming now as couples ended their individual acts and sought other partners. One woman, still wearing her gown across one shoulder, moved into the screen with a large pale rod in her hand, approaching a woman whose rounded bare ass was high in the air, her mouth engaged in pleasuring the man in front of her.

A close up of the rod showed it to be an artificial phallus.

Nick's questions about its usage fled when she slid the rounded tip of her toy against the kneeling woman's nether lips, teasing them apart. She ran it along the inside, obviously toying with the woman's clit, before plunging it deep within her vagina. Several thrusts later the woman was no longer interested in the man's cock, which now hung forlorn and forgotten. He didn't seem to mind though, just moved off to find someone else to suck it, leaving his former lover in the hands of the seductress and her plaything.

Moments later, the woman shuddered deeply and gave a loud shriek, falling to rest on the platform under her. A sly smile crossed the phallus-wielder's face, and she pulled it out, holding it up to the light as if to admire the sheen of womanly fluid coating it. Something about her face was familiar and Nick moved closer to the screen to see it more clearly. She turned and gazed in his direction and again he had that odd feeling of being seen, but this time it didn't go away. Nick pulled the robe even closer around him, and she smiled with disturbing amusement.

Let's see if she finds this funny. Nick stood and pulled open his robe, displaying himself to the screen. The woman's jaw dropped open and she laughed, the source of her merriment obvious as she pointed with her toy phallus at his still hardened member.

Nick rewrapped himself in the robe. Violet was right...he didn't want to walk around with his cock hanging out.

When he turned back to the screen, the woman's face was directly in front of the glass, obscuring the action behind her. He could hear the sex play continue, oblivious to the fact that one of its players was no longer working with the rest of the cast, but instead was doing her own scene with Nick.

She grinned at him. "Narcissus, how nice to see you again."

Shock weakened his knees and he sat in the chair, heavily. "You know me?"

"Certainly." She glanced at the room around him. "You're alone?"

"Yes." He pointed to the screen. "What's going on?"

"An orgy scene, but don't worry, this is only between us. The rest of the cast is having far too good a time to worry about us. A television is usually only for watching, it can't really hear or see you."

Well it was nice to have that confirmed. "So, how is it you can you talk to me."

"Magic, of course. When two people have a connection, there is always magic around."

A connection. "What kind of connection?" he asked warily.

Mock shock rounded her mouth into an O, the joke obvious from the twinkle in her eye. "Why the best kind of connection, Narcissus. Don't you remember me?"

For a moment Nick simply stared at her, then recognition hit him with the force of a falling marble column. Forget her? How could he ever forget? It was the nymph who'd complained so loudly just because he'd preferred to remain aloof than lie with her. "Of course, I remember you…Nemesis!"

The minx laughed from her side of the glass. She tapped the inside with her pink toy, making a pinging sound. "Just Nina, now. You'd be surprised how many people equate my name with something dire."

Flooded by surprised anger, Nick couldn't keep the bitterness out of his voice. "Yeah, well my name has acquired some interesting baggage as well. Either I'm a kind of flower, or a self-absorbed cretin…thanks to you."

Her smile looked satisfied. "Poor Narcissus. Or should I call you Nick? I heard through the Olympian grapevine that you'd been given a brief reprieve. Something about another flower or a deflowering—which was it?"

She'd always been cute with words. "If you're referring to me, yes I'm no longer a virgin. As for the rest…"

"Oh, yes, that was it. She was a flower, too, this woman deserving of your love. Lily, wasn't it?"

"Violet. Not that it should be important to you."

"Everything about you is important to me, Nick. After all, you were my first great love."

"I wouldn't call it love, Nemesis, cursing a man just because he doesn't tumble for you."

The little demoness had the nerve to look contrite. "Wouldn't you, Nick?"

"No I wouldn't. Do you know what I've suffered because of this obsession of yours?"

"I'm sure you've suffered absolute tons, poor baby. That's the reason I wanted to talk to you." Even through the sympathetic tone of her voice, Nick could see her pleasure in his discomfort. Not wanting to remain the butt of her jokes, he picked up the TV remote to turn it off. At least he could shut her up.

Nina tapped the inside of the glass with her fake penis again. "Oh, Nick. Don't touch that dial. Don't you want to hear how I'm going to make it up to you?"

His finger hesitated over the big red button. "There is nothing I want from you."

"Not even to be free of the curse?"

His breath froze in his chest, and for an instant Nick thought he'd turned to stone again. "What are you talking about, Nemesis?"

"Nina, please..." her voice sounded sulky, and Nick groaned inwardly, knowing that tone from before.

"Nina, then. What do you mean 'free of the curse'?"

Smiling she leaned closer to the screen. "I mean I can get you free of the curse, free to be a man for as long as you live. Free to fuck your little flower for the rest of your life."

Nick swallowed hard. "How?"

"I talked to Aphrodite and she agreed that you'd been punished long enough and that she'd let you stay as you are right now."

His breath caught in his throat. It was far too good to be true. "You convinced Aphrodite to let me stay human? Really?"

"Certainly..." She looked indignant. "Do you think I would lie about that?"

"No, of course not. One thing you never were was a liar." A sniveling conniving bitch, perhaps, but she'd always told the truth, her version anyway.

"Well, I'm glad we're agreed. There's just one thing—you have to pass a test. Aphrodite wants to be sure that you learned from your experiences."

"What kind of a test?"

"Oh nothing you can't handle. You need to satisfy a woman. Sexually, of course."

Satisfy a woman? But he'd done that several times already, with Violet. It was far too good to be true. "Is that all?"

Nina had a serpent's smile on her face. "Stand up and do what you did again."

His uneasy feeling returned. Hoping he hadn't understood her, he asked, "Do what again?"

"Stand up and open the robe. Show it to me, Nick."

Slowly he stood and opened Violet's robe, revealing his body. Embarrassed, he couldn't look at the screen for a moment and when he did, he was sorry. Nina's nose pressed hard against the glass and her breath fogged the space beneath. Her eyes were glazed in pure lust as she stared at him. To complete his humiliation, his cock even decided to react to her fevered gaze and rose even further to attention.

"Wow, Nick. Even better than I remembered." She pulled away, eyes bright. "I'm to test you, Nick. Learn as much as you can and then we'll fuck tomorrow night. You satisfy me, and you can stay a man forever. Otherwise it's back to the fountain."

One time with Nina and he could stay human and be with Violet. It sounded wonderful.

It sounded horrible. His cock went limp under the robe.

"Why didn't Aphrodite come and tell me this?"

"I wanted to tell you. The test was my idea after all."

He had trouble finding his voice. "Why are you doing this, Nina?"

Her smile turned wicked. "Because I can, Nick. Because I wanted you and you refused me. Because I'm Nemesis."

Slowly Nick closed the robe. "I want to think about it," he told her, belting it shut.

Her eyes still glowed with subdued lust. "You do that, Nick. Think about it. You'll take the test and pass it, or return to being a statue. I'll contact you tomorrow for your answer."

Once the red button was pushed and the television had faded to black, Nick finally felt the exhaustion that had eluded him earlier. Barely able to keep his eyes open, he turned off the lamp and made his way to the bedroom, and Violet.

She rolled to him as he slipped into the covers, settling herself along his side, the softness of her a reminder of what he stood to gain. He breathed deeply of her special smell, all warm woman. His sex stirred in response.

Could he do that, respond to Nina as he did Violet? From what had happened in the living room, it appeared so. Sex with Violet was wonderful. Could it at least be tolerable with Nina?

If it meant he could stay a man with Violet, surely giving Nina what she wanted would be the right thing to do.

So why did it feel like the wrong thing?

Too many questions and not enough answers to go around. Nick closed his eyes and allowed sleep to claim his mind, letting the argument lapse through slumber.

Chapter Nine

Dawn light filled the window of the room still cold from the night. Violet cuddled close to the large warm figure filling the center of the bed, sighing when his hands slipped along her back to caress her bottom and move it closer to him.

Was there anything sweeter than early morning cuddling? Maybe one thing—early morning loving. She slid her hand down the hard stomach next to her and found an aroused cock rising majestically from the sparse curls at its base. Under her hand it pulsed as she polished it into full erection.

Nick let out a full groan, and pulled her on top of him, one hand finding her sex, stroking it to flame, and driving her into a single-minded passion.

Time to get Nick inside her.

Reaching between them, Violet pulled Nick's cock up to her cleft, and the instant the rounded head felt the opening, he drove upwards, filling her pussy with a single thrust.

Oh, wow. Words came, then fled, as Nick took up a furious pace pistoning into her, his face intense, wild. It was almost as if he didn't see her.

His teeth gritted and he growled. "Is this what you wanted? This? Tell me, woman. You wanted me to fuck you?" He sounded like a man possessed.

Unsure of what to say, more than a little unnerved by his fury, Violet gave in to his passion, rode him as best she could, trying to keep up. Her silence drove him wilder, and he leaned up, capturing her nipple with his teeth, clamping down and pinching it. She cried out at the pain and his eyes flew wide, focused on her.

"Violet!" Immediately he slowed the furious pace, then stopped, keeping her pussy filled but no longer the subject of his furious assault. His face flushed and turned anxious. His gaze dropped to her breast and the nipple he'd bitten. "Did I hurt you?"

"Just a little. Are you always this…energetic in the morning?"

If anything he flushed more. "It's my first morning with a woman, you know that. I was dreaming. Of someone."

"Someone not me?"

He groaned and buried his head between her breasts. "No, not you. Never you."

But what he'd said. "Someone you want to fuck?"

"No…" Nick hesitated. "No, not at all. Just, someone."

"Oh, I see," she said, but she didn't. She looked at Nick's face, the pain in it, the sorrow, and remembered the anger in his voice when he'd spoken. "It's all right, Nick. You don't have to tell me."

"Oh, Violet." He gazed up at her and she once again felt what it was to be loved.

But what they were doing, and without protection. "Nick…we aren't…I mean you don't have a…"

"I know, I know." He pulled out of her, leaving her pussy empty and aching, both from him and for him.

Turning her onto her back, Nick rose to his knees and reached for the bedside drawer she'd found the condoms in last night.

He managed to open the package himself. "This is the only one left," he told her as he slipped it on.

"I guess I better make a stop at the drug store."

Nick's smile warmed her and drove away all her misgivings from before. "I guess you better, my sweet. I plan on using several more in the future."

Covered, he eased his way back in, this time slowly, taking care, making certain she was ready for him. The comparison between now and before was startling, or at least she would have been startled by it if she hadn't been too busy enjoying the way he was sucking on her nipples and tickling her clit while he filled her with his condom-clad cock.

A woman could only focus on so many things at once. Memories of their frantic early-morning coupling faded as Nick created new ones, much more memorable ones in their wake.

Soon Violet rode a crest of pure sensation, Nick raised on his arms above her, her legs wrapped around his as their centers drove together in perfect unison.

"Oh, NICK!" she screamed as the crest dropped out beneath her and she dove headfirst into the pool of passion, dimly aware of Nick's dive right behind her. His voice screamed something inarticulate, and heat blazed between her legs as he climaxed.

Shaking, he lowered himself to his elbows and, voice trembling, whispered into her ear. "I would do anything to be able to do this with you forever, Violet. Anything."

"I know, Nick." She stroked his face, trying to hide her dismay at the thought of him leaving. "I know. I wish there was a way to keep you human."

Hope filled his face. "If I could do something, would it be right? If it meant I could stay with you, be a man forever?"

"What kind of something?"

His face turned guarded. "I can't say…can't talk about it now. But if I could stay, would you want me to?"

Her own hope rising, she nodded. "I'd want you to, Nick. Even if you didn't want to be with me, I'd want you to be free of the curse."

His hands clutched her tightly. "It would be to stay with you, Violet. Don't doubt that, ever. It's you I want always."

"Always is a long time."

"I know what a long time is, Violet. I've waited centuries for someone like you and I know I'll never find another." Still joined, he rolled them, so she rested on top of him. Violet stared into his deep brown eyes with their luxurious lashes and thrilled at the depth of the passion in them.

"I don't want anyone but you, ever. I'd be happy to live with you, grow old with you, and die with you. If I could, would you let me?"

Would she let him? There would never be another man like him. "Yes, I would."

Joy then alarm passed across his face, the emotions chasing each other. Finally resolution filled his features, his eyes turning from warm loving brown to dark stone for a moment.

"Then I'll do everything I can to see it happens," he told her with tight-lipped intensity.

* * * * *

Violet returned from her shower to find Nick glaring at the pathetic array of clothing options she'd left on the bed, the few items she'd found that could possibly fit him.

Apparently the clothing might fit, but little of it appealed to him. He wore a bed sheet wrapped around him, toga style, and she had to admit it suited him far better than the torn t-shirt and open kneed sweatpants he was contemplating.

He held them up. "Violet, where do people get clothing here?"

"Most people buy them."

Interest fired in his face. "At stores? When do they open?"

"Another hour or so…but Nick…" her voice trailed off.

He'd caught the note of hesitation and turned his full attention to her. Putting his hands on her shoulders, he turned her to face him. "What is it, Violet?"

"Much as I'd like to buy you a whole new wardrobe, I can't really afford to. With my job gone, I don't have any money coming in and there isn't very much in my savings."

He chewed on his lower lip for a moment. "You need money to buy me clothes?"

"Well, yes. And money doesn't grow on trees."

Suddenly Nick grinned. Throwing off his bed-sheet garment he donned the sweatpants and t-shirt, adding a pair of flimsy rubber sandals to complete the ensemble.

"Maybe money doesn't grow on trees, but it can sometimes be found there."

Astonished, she followed him to the front door. He gave her a quick kiss before heading out. "I've an errand in the park but I'll be back soon."

She'd completed scrambling eggs and making toast when Nick reappeared through the front door, a small leather backpack in hand. Turning it upside down, he emptied it onto the kitchen table.

Clumps of money fell out, held together with rubber bands, one of which broke as she picked it up, scattering the bills. Most were twenties, several were hundreds. Just in the pile in front of her, Violet counted over two thousand dollars.

"Now we can buy me some clothes," Nick told her proudly.

"Where did this come from?" Violet asked, astonishment vying with alarm. Had Nick held up a convenience store or something?

"From a tree in the park. I overheard some people talking about it, many years ago. It's loot from a robbery I think."

Alarm took center stage. "Loot?" Violet thrust one of the bundles back into the bag. "Nick, take it back. There might be someone looking for it."

"I doubt it, Violet. Not after this many years. I'm not sure, but I believe it was long before I first met you."

She picked up one of the loose bills and examined it. The date was 1966. Another was 1970…a quick survey showed no bills later than 1972. The outside of the leather bag showed a lot of wear and dirt, as if it had been exposed to the elements for a number of years.

"This money has been sitting in a tree since the early seventies?"

Nick nodded. "In a hollow portion. The leather protected the bills."

"I'll say." She held up a hundred dollar bill, still crisp in her fingers. "Outside of the dates, they've aged really well."

"Not unlike me. I've held up pretty well for an old man, right?"

She laughed. She couldn't help it. Nick had brought love, fresh air, and sunlight into her life, and now money, when she desperately needed it.

"Nick, you are the youngest old man I know," she told him, to his delight.

After breakfast she drove them to the biggest discount store in town. If Nick garnered any attention because of his t-shirt and sweatpants mode of dress, it was superceded by his devastating good looks.

They headed for the men's department. Oddly enough for a three-thousand-year-old man made into a three-hundred-year-old statue turned into a man again, Nick had very good instincts when it came to clothing. Violet found she had little to add as he selected good solid basics, a pair of classic khaki pants, black slacks with a built-in crease, and stone-washed denim jeans. For shirts he chose button-down collared shirts, and short sleeved polo's in green, blue, and beige, plus t-shirts. When it came to shoes he found a pair of brightly colored sport shoes and black leather loafers.

On a rack of more expensive items Nick selected a well-constructed black leather jacket that was soft as butter. When Violet saw the price tag, she was grateful for the windfall Nick had collected from the park. When they'd finished counting the money, there was over twenty thousand dollars in small bills to work with, easily enough to handle her bills for a long while, as well as outfit him.

If Nick were going to stay, as he'd implied he might, he'd need clothes and Violet couldn't deny him anything he might want.

Once outer clothing had been covered, socks and underwear followed, Nick leaning toward the bikini style jockey shorts in bright colors. When she asked why that style of underwear, he pointed out that he'd watched her examining the merchandise.

"You spent more time admiring the pictures of the men wearing these. If that's what you want to see when I take off my clothes then that's what I'll wear."

Violet began to feel like it was Christmas and Valentine's Day all rolled into one. With Nick's selections of underwear, she got the candy and could enjoy the bright wrapping it came in as well.

Finally they ended up near men's robes, and Violet watched as Nick selected a robe not unlike hers, bigger of course, and in a dark green. He smiled as he felt its weight and the softness of the terry cloth. "This will do very well."

The bill came to several hundred dollars, but Violet paid it from the tree-fund. The old bills drew no comment at all nor did the fact they paid with cash. Nick pushed the cart to the car and loaded the bags into the back. He was so excited about his new clothes it was all she could do to keep him from changing in the parking lot. As it was, he wore the new jacket and sport shoes home.

A message waited on her answering machine when they came in through the door.

"Ms. Smith…this is Dr. Howard at the Museum of Classical History. We had a cancellation and I was wondering if we could move your appointment up? To eleven-thirty?" There was a brief hesitation. "We really want to speak to you as soon as possible."

The message ended, and Violet stared at the clock. Nearly ten-thirty already! Quickly she called the museum back and confirmed the new time.

She turned to Nick. "I've got to get ready. Please excuse me." She took off for her room, wondering which of her interview outfits was cleanest. Nick followed with his bags, placing them in the corner. As she changed, he did as well, pulling on the khaki pants and the dark-blue button-down shirt, belting it with a leather belt she hadn't remembered going into the bag.

By the time she was dressed, so was he. Violet stared as Nick brushed his hair behind his ears and felt the slight hair that had erupted along his jaw line. It wasn't stubble since he'd never shaved, but it was hair nonetheless.

"Nick, you look wonderful. How do you know so much about clothes?"

His smile was sheepish. "Chauncey and Edgar. They're the gardeners in the park. You wouldn't know it to look at them, but they are forever talking about clothes, the latest styles, what's in and out, what is classic and never a bad idea to buy." He preened at his reflection in the mirror. "I've got to say, I like how I look."

"Careful, Nick. That's how you got into this fix."

His crestfallen expression made her want to take the words back. "I'm sorry, Nick. I didn't think…"

He held up one hand. "No need to apologize, Violet. I know you meant no harm." Chuckling ruefully, he turned his back to the mirror and ran an appraising gaze over her outfit.

His eyebrows beetled into a single line. "Violet, is that what you were planning to wear?"

Startled, she glanced down at the dark skirt, pale-green shirt, and matching sweater. "What's wrong with this? It's one of my best outfits."

Now he frowned and shook his head. "Violet, both the top and the sweater are bulky and hide your shape. It makes you look much heavier than you are—and older as well."

His words were the last thing she'd expected, and Violet couldn't hide the tears in her eyes. She turned from him, and he caught her by the shoulders.

When she looked at him, she saw the instant regret in his face. "I'm sorry, that didn't come out right."

She dashed the tears away with her hand. "I know I'm not the most glamorous woman in the world…"

Nick tilted her head up and gazed deeply into her eyes. "That's not true. You may not be the most fashionable lady around, but you are truly beautiful, Violet. All you need is to wear the clothes that show it." He opened the door to her closet and eyed the contents. "Let me pick something out for you to wear and I'll prove it to you."

She leaned against the doorjamb behind him. "You won't find anything in there that will make me look like a supermodel."

"I don't want you to look like that," he told her as he held up a thin dark-green sweater with small pearl buttons, and examined it with a critical eye. "I just want you to look like the beautiful woman you are. Here, try this on."

She took it from him. "I thought you wanted me to get rid of my layers."

Nick rolled his eyes. "I don't want you wear it *over* your top. Put it on instead."

"Instead!"

"Yes, instead. You hide your body, Violet, and you don't need to. Try it on and you'll see what I mean."

Turning her back, she shrugged off both her shirt and the matching cardigan. Buttoning up the top Nick had picked, Violet's hand trembled. How dare he criticize her clothes? Just because he'd picked out some good-looking outfits for himself didn't make him an expert on women's fashions. Torn between anger and the pain of his derision, she buttoned the sweater all the way to the top then faced him. "Satisfied?" she snarled at him.

Nick's lips pressed into a frown. Seizing her shoulders, he placed her in front of the mirror, taking position behind her. Even through her anger Violet could feel the warmth of him and part of her longed to lean back into it. She closed her eyes as he pulled her closer to him, trying to avoid his pull on her senses.

His hand caressed her shoulder and then fingered the top button, letting it go undone, then did the same to the one below. She felt the warmth of his breath on her ear and heard his deep voice, heavy with emotion. "Look at yourself, Violet. See how lovely you are."

Violet opened her eyes and stared at her reflection. *Could that really be her?* It was her face, Nick's in shadow behind her, but her eyes were wide, cheeks bright with color, her lips looking full and lustrous, half-open as she took deep breathes through her mouth.

The sweater fit her better than she'd imagined, the thinner fabric hugging her curves, clinging to her breasts. Where he'd opened the front, the resulting cleavage gave her a womanly appearance. Not tawdry or seductive, but appealing, plus the open neck drew the eye, making the width of her waist insignificant.

Her mouth dropped open. Nick had been right—she looked beautiful. "I don't believe it," she said, amazed by the change her mirror revealed. The new outfit sent her confidence sky-high. "I look great."

His chuckle rippled through her back. "I told you so, didn't I? You are a lovely woman."

"I still need to lose some weight..."

"Not as much as you think. I mostly think you need to exercise more regularly." One hand slid down her back to rest on her bottom, cupping it and massaging it with sensuous fingers. "'I've heard this kind of activity uses a lot of energy," he said suggestively, his voice setting up waves of sensation in her, most of which landed right into her core.

She pulled herself from his arms. "I need to go, Nick. No time for exercise now."

"I'll go with you."

"No, you shouldn't. What will you do?"

"It's a museum isn't it, of ancient art? They'll have exhibits, maybe even some statues like the ones I was displayed with. Maybe I'll even see someone I know."

She laughed. "Very well. We'll need to hurry, though."

Chapter Ten

Nick leaned against the front desk as Violet spoke to woman sitting behind it, who relayed her presence to the back office.

A moment later the phone rang and the red headed woman answered it. "Dr. Howard will see you now," she said, all the while smiling at Nick, Violet noting her interested gaze running over him as she delivered the message. "Your friend can wait here if he likes." Her smile held a trace of feral attraction. "I'll be happy to keep him company."

Violet narrowed her eyes and was contemplating a retort when Nick spoke up. "Actually, I thought I'd see the museum." He smiled in return. "If that's all right with you."

"Oh, by all means." The redhead reached into a drawer and pulled out a pair of small lapel buttons. "These will get you inside," she purred.

Violet intercepted the items before the other woman could force them into Nick's hand. Leading him aside, she fastened the button to his shirt pocket, using the excuse to be close enough to speak to him softly.

"You might not enjoy this as much as you think. You won't be able to read any of the descriptions."

He considered that. "Perhaps I can get someone else to read them to me?"

"That would seem strange, a man who speaks English as well as you do not being able to read." She glanced around the lobby, her gaze landing on the audio-tour desk and the rack of small players for rental.

She grinned at him. "That's the answer, Nick. I can rent you one of those and show you how to use it. You only need to read numbers to play the correct description of the exhibits, and you already know how to do that."

It took a couple of minutes to teach him the controls, but as always Nick was a quick study. He followed her into the museum until they stopped outside the office door. Nick took his place nearby, in front of a giant urn of Chinese ancestry.

"Good luck," he told her and gave her a quick kiss and a hug.

She hesitated in the doorway, and turned to speak with him once more, but he had already activated the player and was intent on the display nearest the door. Violet watched as he frowned in concentration at the urn. He'd found something to keep him occupied at least.

"Ms. Smith?" She turned to see a portly man with graying hair and narrow spectacles. His smile contrasted with his somewhat harried expression. Seizing her hand, he shook it hard then pulled her into the office. "I'm so glad you could come on short notice...let's go inside and talk."

Hope filled her as she followed him. It sounded like they were desperate...she might have chance at this job after all!

* * * * *

Nick wandered through the cavernous halls, heading for what he hoped would be the Greek and Roman artifacts. As he passed through one doorway, a dusty odor assailed him. He took a deeper breath. Back in a museum again—it even smelled the same as he'd imagined, all old stone and fabric.

A pair of fluted columns as ancient as he was flanked the opening in front of him. Starting his player, he entered the number on the plaque on the wall, and a woman's disembodied voice sounded through the headphones. "Long believed to be part of a temple in Athens before their removal to Rome, these columns have been dated to the Grecian Dark ages, created by local stonemasons..." The explanation droned on, providing more dates, mostly meaningless to Nick. One thing did attract his attention, though. At the bottom of the left column was a small set of letters, chipped into the base.

Nick smiled. It was a name of the stonemason who'd carved the columns, someone he'd met once. The man had been an Ionian who'd never ventured anywhere near Athens. The explanation on the tape was wrong, the dates mixed up. The Grecian name was there for the entire world to see but only he had the eyes to view it.

This discovery filled him with curiosity. What other mistakes could he find? Feeling as if he ventured on a treasure hunt, Nick explored the exhibits, thrilled with each new mistake.

There really was something he could offer the people of this time! If he could learn to read English, he'd be more than able to demonstrate his proficiency as a classical scholar, with or without a formal education. The possibilities filled him with something he'd not experienced in a long time.

Hope. Hope of a future, in this world, with his lovely Violet.

Eventually he found another room, filled with statuary, some old, some less so. One caught his attention, a nymph peeking from behind a tree, her expression vivid with longing, her gaze fixed on something only she could see. Her mouth hung open as if she intended to speak, the words frozen on her tongue. He stepped closer to examine the pensive face, wondering if he really recognized her. He'd been joking with Violet earlier when he'd spoke of meeting people he knew, but here was someone familiar.

"Echo, of course." Nick tore his headphones off and turned. Behind him stood Nemesis—that is, Nina—the quiet in her voice almost hiding her anger. "My sister nymph, if you remember—and another of your 'conquests'."

Conquest. Well, not really. "I remember her. She was so shy she wouldn't speak to me, just answer me with my own words."

"That was the story. She became a shadow of herself and faded away. All that was left of her was her voice, calling endlessly. I still hear her sometimes."

Nick shook his head, unexpected sorrow filling him. "Can she be freed, the way I was?"

She shrugged. "Maybe, eventually. She needs to want her liberty, and so far she hasn't. Not like you."

Catching the meaningful tone in her voice, Nick turned his attention to her. He took in Nina's appearance, the lean figure dressed in a sheath dress far too short and trendy for a museum on a weekday afternoon. With her long black hair swept up in a loose French twist, she might have stepped out of a fashion magazine.

It was unnerving to see her in the flesh. On the television screen it had been easier to ignore her innate sexuality, but in person it was impossible. The woman fairly screamed sex even without a phallus in her hand.

She took his arm and pulled him down an aisle, between two statuary groups. Rubbing against him, she purred into his face. "I'm so looking forward to our little meeting, lover. I can hardly wait until this evening."

"I'm sure you can't." Nick tried to pull away and put some distance between them. Having to put up with this woman was taking a toll. It would feel so good to simply dump the bitch on her rear.

But if he did...he wouldn't be allowed to stay with Violet. For his ladylove, he'd do anything.

Even put up with Nemesis...that is, Nina.

Even have sex with her? Yes, if that's what would free him.

She bit down on his knuckles and he pulled his hand away. "Nina, how do I know that you're telling the truth, that if we have sex I'll be set free?"

Retreating, she glared at him. "Do you think I'd dare lie to you, promising the gods' forgiveness in exchange for a little hanky panky? Do I look stupid, Nick? If I hadn't gotten the power-that-be's okay on this, there is no way I'd come to you with this proposition." She shuddered. "They'd be sure to take away my privileges as an immortal spirit...and that's not something you'd wish on your worst enemy!"

He had to admit she was right. To sneak something of this magnitude past the gods was an act of insanity, one thing he'd never accuse her of. Still, he couldn't let it go that easily. "You're Nemesis, you're anyone's worst enemy."

She looked offended. "Hey, everyone's got a part to play, *Narcissus,* even you. That whole staring into a pond thing was a great object lesson for the terminally self-absorbed. The question is, have you really gone beyond it? Can you do what needs to be done to earn your redemption?"

Hesitation wasn't an option. "I have, Nina. Really. I'll do anything to stay with Violet."

Mollified, she gave him a feral grin. "Very well. Meet me tonight, in the park, alone. There is a shed used by the gardeners that will be unlocked and unguarded. It's actually kind of romantic if you don't mind the smell of fertilizer. Be there at two a.m. and we'll see what we can do to absolve you. I promise, I'll make it worth your while…in more ways than one."

It sounded like a fate worse than death—but death wasn't an option anyway. Instead of dying, he'd return to stone, to stare endlessly at his reflection. If he was to retain his current humanity he had to do what she wanted.

"Okay," he said reluctantly. "Whatever you say."

"Whatever who says?" Violet's voice caught his attention and Nick twisted in Nina's hold to face his sweetheart.

His sweetheart was hopping mad at him. Arms folded, she tapped one foot meaningfully, staring at the hand Nina still had clamped to his forearm.

"Who's this, Nick?"

He pulled away from Nina. "Just someone I know, Violet."

"A friend? Here? I didn't think you knew anyone."

"Someone from a long time ago." Nina's hand had disappeared, and when Nick looked around, so had the woman herself. Melted into thin air, it seemed, and inwardly he breathed a sigh of relief. Nina's sudden disappearance apparently registered with Violet, who looked around with some consternation. "Where did she go?"

Best to distract her. "Violet…did you get the job?"

To his surprise the subterfuge worked. Violet's eyes lit up, and she smiled broadly. Grabbing his hands, she pulled them into the warm mounds of her breasts. Nick resisted a groan at their softness.

"I did, Nick. I start next Monday. They're even paying me half-again the salary I was making before. It's so wonderful!"

"I'm so glad, Violet. You deserve it."

Nina apparently forgotten, she continued to bubble with excitement. "I owe it to you, Nick. He told me that the minute he saw me he knew I was just what they were looking for. It was the outfit you picked out for me…it made me look like an administrator."

"You are an administrator…and a very good one."

"But I didn't look like one, before. I didn't know what was missing, but it was the way I was dressing." Throwing her arms around him, Violet hugged Nick. "You made a big difference Nick. Really."

She cuddled in close and Nick held her, relishing her loving nature. His woman, his for all time after tonight.

After making love to another woman.

He pulled her closer and buried his face in her hair. That's what it came down to, doing with Nina what he'd willingly done with Violet. How hard could it be to have sex with a woman he didn't really want? Men did it all the time.

He surely could do it…even now his cock hardened at the idea of making love…to someone…anyone…Violet, Nina…what was the difference? Both were female, both offered the same parts.

There was even a part of him that acknowledged that Nina was the physically more attractive of the two.

But that didn't matter. He was in love with Violet and that made a big difference. To make love without love, could that be done?

Of course it could. But was it desirable?

Violet buried her head deeper into his chest. "Oh, Nick. I hope you're right, I hope you can stay with me. It would be terrible to give you up now."

He ran his hands along her back, pressing her closer. It didn't matter what was right or wrong or what he desired. He wanted to stay human and with Violet, and to accomplish that he'd do anything.

Even have sex with Nina, his Nemesis of so long ago. It wasn't a question or an option. It was an imperative.

There was no choice.

Violet felt so wonderful in his arms. He had to keep her close and smell her earthy aroma, the scent of woman and the future. To live with Violet, love Violet, make love to Violet. To be her husband and see her swell with his child. Every moment with her was more poignant than the last.

How could he possibly give her up? Answer—he couldn't.

The museum suddenly seemed more closed in than ever, full of old objects, things from a past he no longer wanted to be part of. He needed to get away from it, out in the open where there were living things around. Go where there was life.

He tilted her face to meet his gaze. "Violet, let's go to the park. I want to walk outside for a while."

Chapter Eleven

There was a street fair on the way to the park. Nick walked with Violet down the long stretch of booths featuring all kinds of homemade arts and crafts. The more things changed, the more they stayed the same. If he ignored the cars passing in the street and the clothes the people wore, many of the handmade items displayed could have easily been from his own time.

Distracted by a seller of woolen shawls in bright colors, Violet lagged behind, giving Nick a chance to examine the wares of a jeweler whose display of necklaces and earrings had caught his attention. He discovered the man's rings, delicate gold hoops with intricate carvings. One in particular took his fancy, gold and silver combined, the delicate tracery that of small flowers.

He took a closer look. *Violets*—that what they were, small five-petal flowers, detailed with remarkable skill. Holding the ring up, Nick asked the price, as quietly as he could. It was expensive, but thanks to the money he'd found in the park he could afford it. He quickly paid the man and slipped the ring into his pocket before Violet rejoined him.

He wanted to ask Violet to be his wife and if he remembered the ritual properly from having overheard it in the park, a ring was a vital part of the procedure.

They found another booth that sold drinks and food, and Nick sampled his first hotdog with extra mustard and relish. He rolled his eyes at the mixture of smoky, salty meat and sharply flavored mustard. Wonderful food. It was going to be so great to be a man and be able to eat hotdogs every day.

After lunch they turned toward the park and wandered the narrow pathways. The park was as beautiful as Violet had ever seen it on a fall day. Pine and fir trees kept their green while their deciduous brothers were a riot of color. Leaves, gold and red, lay scattered upon the broad carpet of grass, children running through them, kicking them high in the air. Overhead the sky was a deep blue, white clouds floating across it in ever changing patterns. Last night's rain was a distant memory, the sun having dried the pathways and heated the air to a temperature closer to that of summer than winter.

As they passed near the now statue-less fountain, Violet noticed yellow caution tape around the outside and several people arguing over what had happened. Nick swerved to avoid getting too close, heading them toward the children's playground. On a nearby bench, she saw Helen holding the latest in a series of books that appealed to both adults and younger readers. She was reading aloud to a little girl, maybe six years old, sitting in her father's lap. While the child's rapt attention was on the book, the man seemed far more interested in the reader.

"I guess Helen took your advice, Nick," Violet told him softly.

He smiled in return. "Perhaps your friend Marge will hunt down the duck feeder. I have a feeling they might have a lot in common."

They walked on, and Violet kept her hand looped through Nick's arm, appreciating the security of his strong arm. As other people passed she noticed how many of the women turned to cast an interested glance in Nick's direction. He was such a handsome man. She tried to ignore the puzzled looks several of the women gave her, as if she had no business being on Nick's arm.

What business was it of theirs if he was in love with her? She had every bit as much a right to love as anyone...even if she was a few pounds overweight and lacked the height and figure of so many other women.

Nick wanted her, not them. He'd come to life to become her lover, and even now had a plan to stay with her forever. Could anyone else say that?

No, they couldn't. Nick had loved her when he was made of stone.

But he wasn't made of stone any longer. A strikingly beautiful woman walked by, and Nick turned his head to follow her progress as she passed. A fleeting distraction for him, nothing more...he immediately returned to smile into her face, but she'd noticed his brief defection.

*Tall, thin, and gorgeous. Like that woman who'd been with Nick at the museum...*Violet's heart sank. That black-haired beauty had been all of that, her hands all over Nick, as if claiming him for her own. And he hadn't seemed to mind that woman's touch, either. A woman who'd disappeared, she suddenly remembered, and a chill ran through her.

"You feeling all right?" Nick's deep brown eyes gazed into hers, with such a mix of love and desire that Violet squashed the jealousy and fear that had risen. How could she possibly doubt Nick?

"I'm fine. Just a little cold, I guess." She blamed the weather instead of her own insecurities.

Mischief blossomed in his eyes. "Perhaps we should find a place to warm up." He pulled her off the path and toward a set of buildings toward the back of the park. "Come with me, I've got somewhere in mind."

* * * * *

The gardener's shed. It loomed in front of them, the dark green walls designed to fade into the park's background and be unnoticeable to the patrons who frequented the grounds nearby. The place looked deserted, the gardeners having finished their work hours ago.

It was the location where he was to meet Nina later tonight and buy his future with his body. Smiling, Nick pulled Violet around to the door. He'd test out the suitability of it as a trysting place with his own lady first.

"What do you have in mind, Nick?" Violet's soft voice was tentative, but there was a note of intrigue as well. He suppressed a laugh…he was making quite an adventurer out of his shy little flower.

Inside it was dark, but he could make out the high potting tables, crowded with plants. In the corners were stacked large bags of soil and fertilizer, lending an earthy smell to the room. Nick took a deep breath. After the museum's atmosphere of age and decay, the potting shed smelled wonderful.

Violet wrinkled her nose. "It stinks in here."

He laughed. "I don't think so. It smells alive." He swept her up and sat her on the top of one of the tables. Burying his nose in her hair, he took a deep breath. "It smells just like you."

Playfully she swatted at his hand, which had disappeared under her shirt. "I do NOT smell like fertilizer."

He nuzzled her in response. "Your scent is that of warm earth under a summer sun, and I love you for it." No longer content to smell her skin, he now tasted it, savoring her sweetness, running his teeth and tongue down the side of her neck. His hand slid up under her bra and kneaded her breast, feeling the hard pebble of her nipple spring to attention.

Inside his pants his cock came to attention as well.

One problem. They still hadn't gone to the pharmacy and he had none of the rubber sheaths they'd come to depend on. Perhaps they could come up with another way to have sex, one that wouldn't risk pregnancy.

He slid his hands under her skirt, hiking it up to give him easier access. Under the silky feel of her tights, her underwear had dampened, but the heavy nylon barrier proved to be effective in giving his fingers no access.

He muttered his frustration and heard Violet's short laugh. "I guess that's why women wear stockings and garter belts, even if pantyhose is more convenient." She lifted her rear and allowed him to pull the top of the offending garment down to her thighs, conveniently taking her underwear with it. Immediately he took advantage and his fingers delved deep within her, fondling the folds and rubbing his palm against her clit. Violet clung to him, mouth open and eyes glazed as the first tremblings ran through her body.

Nick drove his fingers further into her sheath, allowing one to caress the tiny puckered opening further back. Violet gasped but made no complaint as he massaged all of her parts, first gently, then more insistently. Instead she laid her head on his shoulder and leaned into his hand.

She shuddered and a long moan began. Nick covered her open mouth with his, swallowing Violet's orgasmic cry, to keep its sound within the shed. She collapsed against him, whimpering her delight.

His cock ached in near pain, and he wanted to beg for relief. It felt like it could poke through the fabric of his clothes all by itself.

Violet's breaths still came in short gasps, her face flushed with arousal. "Nick, we aren't prepared for this..." Then her eyes widened and she smiled. "On the other hand, there's one thing I haven't done for you."

She jumped off the table. Kneeling before him and reaching for his belt, she gave him a seductive look that stopped his breath. As the belt buckle slipped free and his zipper came down, Nick realized that he was no longer in charge of the seduction. His shy little woman was absolutely taking the lead.

Then her mouth closed over his shaft and he lost all ability to reason.

Violet sucked on the head of his cock, her lips warm, her mouth damp and inviting. It was different from the first time she'd taken him in her mouth, in the bedroom when she'd been still tentative. Now she was so sure. There was nothing less than total enthusiasm here, soft liquid sounds coming from her, barely registering over the other feelings flooding through him.

As if of their own volition, his hands found purchase around her head, and held her as she slid up and down his shaft. *Gods...what a sensation!* He didn't want her to stop...no, not at all...but if she didn't...

"Violet, I don't think I can hold back," he managed to get out between teeth clenched so tight they felt like they might crack.

She paused and pulled off him, staring up at him, eyes wide with…what? Laughter? Amazement? Her hand still stroked his shaft, the other slipping deeper into his pants to capture and fondle his balls. He groaned under her gentle torture.

"Nick, I'm afraid that's the point of a blow job. I don't want you to hold back…you're supposed to come."

He blinked. "Oh…uh…okay."

Shaking her head and chuckling, Violet ran her tongue along the narrow cleft, gathering the beaded pre-cum there. She licked her lips. "Tastes wonderful so far, Nick. Can't wait for the rest."

Nick suppressed an undignified whimper. The sight of his cock disappearing into her mouth again was too much. He couldn't watch any longer or he'd explode. Closing his eyes, he gave himself up to her.

Within moments he gave up the rest, too. Some part of him remembered their location and the people outside the building, the distant shouts of children, and it made him swallow his cry as his organ pulsed in Violet's mouth, spending his seed where it would do no harm. Dimly he was aware of her leaning against him and swallowing his semen.

Then he tugged her to her feet and into his arms. His mouth covered hers and his kiss wasn't gentle, but savage, possessive. He could still taste himself in her mouth, the sweet-sour flavor lingering on her tongue.

He knew what they'd done before had been intimate, but this was a gift, precious, the act of a loving woman for a man she cared for. Violet was his woman. Now and always, his.

Gathering her closer with one arm, Nick reached into his pocket, found the ring he'd purchased before. He held it before her and saw the look of recognition and wonder in her eyes.

"Violet, I want to stay with you, always. Will you be my wife?"

Her hand shook as she took the ring and slipped it onto her finger. It fit, perfectly.

Her eyes were shining as she smiled into his face. "Yes, Nick, I will."

Chapter Twelve

They stopped at the drugstore on the way home and picked up much-needed supplies from the family planning department. Violet and Nick lingered near the counter for a long time, debating textures and sizes, laughing over the notion of flavorings. Ultimately they agreed on a large box of a familiar brand, promising themselves a more adventurous selection later.

Secretly, Violet considered seeing her doctor and asking about alternatives, a diaphragm or the pill, at least for a while. If she was going to be Nick's wife, she wanted to eliminate needing to think about protection every time.

She also led him to the book section and found a children's book with simple language. Tonight they'd start teaching Nick to read and write.

A stop at the grocery netted steak, potatoes, and the makings of a salad. Violet watched as Nick wandered the wine aisle, examining the bottles with an astonished and pleased expression. He finally settled on a rich merlot that one of the store clerks recommended.

Violet fingered the lovely silver and gold ring on her finger. How could she have possibly gotten this lucky? Twenty-four hours ago she'd been at the depths of despair, and now she couldn't imagine herself any happier. She collected a package of chocolate chip cookies and added it to their cart, smiling as Nick questioned her about them.

"Trust me, Nick, you're going to love them," she told him.

Dinner was a celebration—of Violet's new job, of Nick's freedom from his curse, and most of all of their future, the two of them engaged to be married.

It had all happened so quickly, but Violet was too happy to question it. After all, there were ancient gods—and goddesses—on her side. Why shouldn't she have a run of good luck?

All through the meal they stared at each other, barely able to keep their hands on their forks and not reach for the other's body. The salad was crisp, the dressing tangy, the potatoes had baked to perfection. The steak, stuck under the broiler until it no longer bled pink, filled their mouths with rich meaty flavor. Nick toasted the grocery clerk who'd helped him pick the wine and called him a genius, promising to get the young man's name next time they were there.

It was one of the best meals Violet had ever eaten…and she barely noticed any of it, so engrossed was she in the fire in Nick's eyes, the desire she felt for him in return.

They never got to dessert. As soon as the last of dinner was consumed, Nick swept her out of her seat and carried her to the bedroom.

* * * * *

Nick captured Violet's mouth as they passed through the door, and before they reached the bed he couldn't think of anything but how much he wanted her. So warm, so responsive. She filled him with need, the need to be close to her, to fill her, to possess her.

She'd agreed to become his wife. A vision of the future appeared to him, of Violet pregnant with his child, her loving face radiant with impending motherhood, but still his lover. It was going to come true…all of it!

They reached the bed and he placed her on her feet, the better to free his hands. He needed her naked, and didn't wish to wait for her to disrobe. He'd do that duty, if only to make sure it was done as soon as possible. Reaching for her sweater, he unbuttoned it, one button at a time, revealing the simple bra that supported her full breasts. White cotton, unadorned by lace or frills.

Violet deserved better than such simple underwear. Even last night's pink silk panties hadn't been fancy, not that he'd cared at the time. Soon he would take her to a lingerie shop and insist she buy something more appropriate to showcase her beauty.

In the meantime he unhooked her bra and discarded it, letting her lovely globes spill into his hands. She moaned her approval as he played with them, his mouth trailing kisses along her neck. When she reached for the buttons on his shirt, he stepped back and let her do the job.

Sure, he could have done it faster, but fast wasn't always better. When she got the garment off and ran her fingers down his chest, he groaned at the feel of her hands, the anticipation as she'd removed his shirt making the sensation more poignant.

He groaned again. Sex tonight was going to be wonderful.

Her skirt came off next, followed by the pantyhose. As he pulled them from her, he thought about what she'd said in the gardener's shed about stockings and garter belts. *Something else to add to his shopping list.* Easier access to her sweet center was high priority.

Once naked, Violet slipped onto the bed and watched him as he pulled off his pants. The look in her eyes made him feel powerful, invincible. He knew what he wanted and knew he could have it just by reaching out for it.

What he wanted was her, so out he reached. Violet put her hand in his and drew him onto the bed beside her.

His cock stiffened as he kissed her and played with her breasts, then hardened more when she moaned while he fed on the sweet nectar between her legs. By the time she bent to take him into her mouth, he was aching for her touch, for relief from the tension. It was all he could do to not explode in her mouth like an untried boy.

Nick wouldn't do that, not this time. When he came, it would be deep inside her with her sheath pulsating around him, milking the semen from his body. He pulled her from his cock and forced her mouth to his, tasting a little of himself on her tongue.

Remembering his favorite of the positions he'd seen in last night's TV, he turned her away from him, urging her onto her knees. She went willingly, as eager for the new experience as he was.

Belatedly he remembered the need for protection and reached to open the bedside table drawer and grab a condom from the new box. But the drawer didn't hold what he was looking for and he realized he'd opened the wrong one. Instead of finding a cardboard box, a hard, round smoothness came into his hand. Clasping it, Nick lifted the surprising object from its hiding place.

He gaped. *The last time he'd seen one of these, it had been in Nina's hand!* Long, and thick, made of pink plastic embedded with molded veins, the artificial penis was at least the size of his cock…maybe bigger.

"Nick?" Obviously sensing some change, Violet turned her head, and sat up abruptly, flushing when she saw what he held. "Oh…dear…" she stammered, her cheeks bright pink.

"Violet…what…why…" He waved it at her.

Her response was an embarrassed giggle that grew louder as it punctuated her words. "It's a vibrator. It was a present—for my birthday last year—from my women's group." She convulsed with laughter. "They said if that's all I needed Gary for, I would be better off with one of my own!"

Nick had to laugh. The ladies certainly had that right. He found a small switch on the bottom and moved it, and immediately the thing came to life. It vibrated his hand, nearly causing Nick to drop it. Violet's giggle grew more nervous at the sound.

Remembering Nina's toy on the television last night, and the response of the woman she'd used it on, Nick wondered if Violet would have the same reaction. Not that he wanted her to enjoy a toy better than his equipment…but it wouldn't hurt to experiment.

"I want to try something, Violet."

Her gaze darted to the vibrator. "With that? I've never used it, Nick."

"It's all right. I know what to do. Just lie back and trust me."

Eyes wide, she obeyed, her nervousness palpable. Remembering how skillfully Nina had applied her version, Nick ran the vibrating head across her nipples, wringing a quick whimper of pleasure from her.

Encouraged, Nick repeated the action, careful not to press too hard and over-stimulate her. Violet closed her eyes and trembled as he slid it along her belly, leading to the tender places of her womanhood. Moments later she clutched the sheets when he let it glide past her soft mound and into the folds that surrounded her clit. Using the utmost care, he gently caressed her most sensitive parts, letting the vibration do the work rather than the movement of the phallus.

Violet's appreciative moans stated the toy's effectiveness. When he pulled it away, her eyes opened in dismay. "Don't stop," she begged.

Grinning, Nick held it out. "You do it, Violet. I've something to take care of."

"But I told you, I never—" she began, flustered.

"Then I'll enjoy it all the more, watching you play with it for the first time."

Her cheeks grew pinker than ever, but she took it from him. Shyly she placed the vibrating head just outside of her woman's mound, the soft curls shivering in sympathy. Tentatively at first, then with more enthusiasm, Violet pushed the artificial cock across her opening, letting it linger on her clit. Repeating the action, her head flew back and she gave several sharp cries.

For a few moments Nick enjoyed the sight of his woman pleasuring herself, until he remembered what he'd been looking for when he'd found her toy. He tried another drawer and found the condoms, tearing the side of the box in his hurry to get one of the small packages. He was more careful when it came to opening the foil itself, not wishing to damage the sheath within.

How much longer did he need to wear one of these? Now that Violet had agreed to become his wife, surely he could persuade her to have his child. Maybe not immediately…but sometime soon. In the meantime he rolled the thin rubber into place.

Cock covered, he leaned over Violet and took his buzzing competition from her. Switching it off, he put it out of her reach. "My turn," he told her with a meaningful grin.

Her attitude was sweet anticipation as she allowed him to turn her again onto her hands and knees, her ass high in the air and waiting for him. Enfolding her in his arms, Nick positioned his cock to enter her from behind. As soon as his cock felt her narrow slit, he pushed inside, his way eased by the heavy sexual dew accumulated there. The vibrator had done its work in preparing Violet for him…only the faintest moan indicated that she wasn't immediately ready for him.

Even so, her sheath was tight around him and Nick had to hold himself from an instant climax as her pussy clutched at him, milking his cock. He pulled back and pushed forward again, making the stroke easy. Holding her around the waist, he guided her to move with him, setting the pace slow at first, only speeding up as her own passion began to drive her. Soft moans grew more earnest as she reached the first stages of pleasure.

Incipient shudders ran down her back, and Nick drove harder into her. He reached around and found her breasts, swinging in time with their undulating bodies. Their heaviness filled his hands, and the tips were pebble hard against his palms. He tweaked them and was rewarded by Violet bucking against him, her cunt clutching his cock. Leaving one hand to toy with her nipples, his fingers found the swollen nub between her legs and rubbed it in time with his thrusts.

Violet stiffened and cried out beneath him. "Nick, more. Please."

Her legs widened to give him deeper access and he took full advantage to sink further into her. One hand rested on her belly, and he could almost feel the end of his cock through the skin as it slammed into her. One thrust, then two, then four, then ten…he kept up the pounding until it seemed each plunge into her was in time with his raging heartbeat. Within him tension built, with every thrust into his lover's body.

Violet shuddered again, another level of passion reached, and a drawn-out moan came from her. Nick groaned his own answer as she rocked back into him, taking all of him and then some, taking the pace up herself as she drove to an ultimate climax. His fingers dug into her waist and held on, no longer able to control either Violet or his own movements.

With a cry he gave up the battle and spasmed, once, twice, his cock pulsing and spilling seed to be caught in its rubber container, his mind soaring on passion's wings. Violet collapsed forward onto the bed and Nick enfolded her in his arms, breathing heavily into her neck. He fell to his side and cradled her close.

They lay together, lungs struggling to recover forgotten breaths. Violet's back was warm against his chest and her hair a soft fluff under his cheek. He rubbed through it to find the soft skin of her neck, so he could nuzzle his woman, his lover, soon to be his wife.

She would be his wife until death parted them. By giving up his existence as a statue, he'd be giving up immortality, to choose a single life of limited duration, to choose sickness, aging, and eventual death.

His choice would be to live one life with warm, loving Violet by his side, as opposed to spending an eternity as cold stone. In the afterlife to come they'd walk together as they did in this one.

It was a bargain if ever he heard one.

Nick nuzzled Violet's shoulder, the flame of passion banked for the moment. Not for long, he could tell. Soon he'd want her again.

But for now it was enough just to hold her. "So, what else do people do when they aren't making love?"

She laughed. "You are forever asking that."

"I want to know. What else do they do?"

"Oh, watch TV. Talk, read."

"I can't read."

Her eyebrows wriggled mischievously. "Why don't we change that? We could start with your first reading and writing lesson."

He pulled her closer and nibbled on her ear. He was too full of good food, great wine, and warm woman to want to study right now. "Maybe later."

"How much later?" Violet asked, her voice teasing. In answer he kissed her. As always, her lips ensnared him. He couldn't get enough of them, as if they held a drug he'd become dependent on. Maybe there was something to that, that he craved Violet, her lips and mouth, the soft mounds of her breasts, the sweetness of the cleft between her legs. He could never get enough of that.

Sex with Violet could become habit forming. A shame that...to become addicted to love.

He hoped he never found a cure.

His sex stirred again and Nick glanced at the clock. He had hours yet before he had to meet Nina. Perhaps they had time for more lovemaking, this time slower. He reached one hand for her breast. She gazed back at him in blissful anticipation.

The distant sound of the doorbell broke the spell and pulling out of his arms, Violet groaned and got to her feet. "I'll see who it is," she said, grabbing her robe off the floor as she headed out of the room.

Nick leaned back on the pillow, intending to wait for her. Then he heard Gary's voice.

Barely managing to tie his own robe before leaving the bedroom, Nick charged toward the front of the house. The other man had managed to insert himself into the front doorway, preventing Violet from closing the front door without risking harm to the man's foot.

Nick suppressed a growl. Left up to him, Gary would already be outside, nursing an injured member. He'd no compulsions about sparing the man's feelings…or toes.

Gary leaned against the door and smiled. "Hey, babe. I heard you got a job over at the museum. Nice going. According to the receptionist, Marilyn, it's a big promotion for you. I thought I'd stop by and see if you wanted to celebrate." Nick bristled as the other man ran a lecherous gaze over Violet's body. "I see you're dressed for it."

She blushed, pulling back from him, and it was all Nick could do to not rush forward and punch the man in his foul-minded mouth. Instead he sauntered into the room, catching Gary's attention.

The other man straightened, his eyes narrowing. "Well, I see your friend is still here." His gaze ran up and down the new robe. "Managed to find something new to wear, as well. Nice. Better than my old cast-offs. I guess Violet didn't mind outfitting you after all." He glared down into her face. "Not as broke as you claimed to be."

"Gary, I think you should go."

"Why, was I interrupting something?" he said nastily. "I know your boyfriend was only supposed to be around a couple days—"

Nick put a possessive arm around Violet's shoulders. "Not anymore. I'm planning on being here a very long time."

Gary took a belligerent stance, breathing heavily, and Nick could smell alcohol on his breath. "Oh, really?"

"Really." He glared at the man over Violet's head. "She's promised to be my wife."

"Your WIFE!" Astonishment crossed the other man's face and he turned on Violet. "But you barely know this guy! You can't be serious."

"I know him well enough to love him, Gary. And he loves me in return."

Gary's eyes flickered from one to the other. "I don't believe it. You're an idiot to trust him. This guy'll be off as soon as he gets tired of you."

Fury filled Nick. "Why, because that's what you did? I love Violet and I'll never hurt her."

Violet smiled at him then turned to Gary. "You need to leave now and I don't want you coming back anymore, either. We're finished and we have been since you walked out last week."

Something nasty scooted across the man's face. "Okay, I guess you know best. I wish you luck."

Nick didn't trust the man, and was happy to see the door closed in his face.

Violet gave him a troubled look. "I'm sorry about that, Nick. Gary always seems to be turning up at the wrong time and saying something awful."

He collected her into his arms. "He doesn't matter, Violet, not at all. I'm so happy to be staying. I love being here, enjoying wine, warm baths, tuna with noodles…" He pulled her closer and nuzzled her. "You…"

Violet laughed. "I didn't think you were ready to make love again."

His voice was muffled by her neck. "I'm not just yet. But I can still hold you." He kissed her, tasting her mouth with his tongue. "What else do lovers do, Violet…"

"When they aren't making love?" She finished for him. "Well, sometimes they dance."

"I don't know how to do your kind of dancing." He sounded contrite, as if it was somehow his fault that he'd been unable to learn to dance during the past three hundred years.

"It's easy. I'll show you." Leaving his arms, Violet moved to her small stereo and selected a slow dance CD by a woman artist she was fond of. The sultry sound of the first track began, the low wail of a saxophone beginning the melody while the drums and bass provided a rhythm perfect for his lesson. Nick would have no problem moving to this music.

He smiled as the deep sultry voice of the singer began her lament of a short-time love. "I like this. It's different from the music I usually hear. Sometimes a young person will bring their music box to the park, but the sound is harsher and I can't understand the words." He tilted his head, his smile fading. "I know just what she's saying."

The need to clear the sadness from his eyes was overwhelming and Violet pulled him to the middle of the room, where there was room to move. "Don't worry about the words, Nick. We'll make up our own lyrics for the song."

Swaying back and forth, she led him until he caught the gist of their movement and took over, feet shuffling to the rhythm of the music, his arms locked around her back, her head tucked under his chin. His possessive hold felt wonderful, and for the first time in years, Violet felt like she belonged to someone, that someone cared for her. She leaned into the warmth of his arms, his breath hot against her cheek.

Violet allowed her hands free play over his chest as they moved together, the sculpted muscles flexing against her. Sliding her hands around his back, she settled on his waist, hugging him the way he hugged her.

As she'd expected, Nick took to dancing the way he'd taken to making love, with a natural skill, and passion that went beyond normal measurement.

Violet began to suspect something. When Affrodite, or whatever her name was, had interfered with his punishment and turned Narcissus into Nick, a human man, he'd been created to be perfect for making love—for making love to her. He might seem to be ignorant in the most basic things, but instinctively he knew everything he needed to make her come alive in his arms.

How could he be anything but wonderful at close dancing? She leaned into the deep V of the robe, filling her lungs with his warm, sexy smell, the scent of man mixed with sweat, the smell of sex from their earlier encounter. For a moment Violet wondered if Gary had noticed it, that Nick smelled of love well made.

Maybe he had. Violet wondered at how that thought didn't dismay her the way she'd expected it to. But then, not much was dismaying her this evening.

Nick led her around the living room, their bodies locked together, his arms as much supportive as securing. He held her body captive to his wants, his desires, just as her heart was captive.

It had been a long time since Violet had felt something like this, a long time of being under the thrall of a man who cared little for her, and less for how she felt. Nick did care…about her, about her needs, her desires.

Nick cared about her the way she cared about him.

She loved him. He behaved as if he loved her.

She could never let him go.

The song ended, the singer ending on a low, sultry note that left no doubt as to the intention of the song. It was a CD Violet had picked up shortly before Gary had left, and he'd ridiculed her taste in buying it.

Of course he had. It was a CD of love songs and Gary had never been in love.

"I love this music," Nick whispered, the breath from his mouth near her neck teasing her skin like a soft breeze.

It was the music of love. Nick would take to it like a duck to water. She should have known when Gary hadn't liked it, that there was something wrong between them.

But Nick had known all along that she and Gary were doomed. Why was that? Could Nick have read Gary's heart, and known it wasn't full of love for her?

Or had it just been wishful thinking on his part, that no man, Gary or anyone else, could ever be the right man for her?

Only Nick was the right man.

Perhaps that was it. She could feel his longing, his need for her, in the gentle strength of his arms, in the deep breaths he took as he held her close, in the fierce pounding of his heart…and in the hardness of his cock, pressed firmly against her.

Once more Nick was hard, ready for sex. Ready to fuck. No, not fuck. Ready to make love.

And so was she.

The next tune from the stereo was faster than the first, and Nick picked up the tempo to glide them across the room. When she looked up into his face, Violet saw the strain she was putting on him, the need he was keeping under control. She ground herself against him, and heard his gasp.

"Violet!" Astonishment colored his eyes, his cheeks pink and it was all she could do to keep from laughing at his embarrassment. He was there to show her love, but she had a few lessons for him as well.

"Come on, Nick," Violet crooned. "We both know what comes next."

He froze in place, ignoring the music still coming from the stereo, consternation in his face. "I don't want tonight to be only about sex, Violet."

She pressed her hand against his face. "It won't be. But that doesn't mean we shouldn't be taking advantage of the situation."

He smiled. "This is what I've come to show you, Violet. How to give in to your hunger for love."

Once more they were engaged in a meeting of tongues and lips, a kiss that again blew away all of her preconceptions of what kissing was about.

"Violet, I can't get enough of you." His voice sounded harsh, strained in her ears. "All I want is to make love to you, right this minute."

Mischief blossomed in her. She pulled him to the wall and raised her legs to wrap around his waist. "Well, then, what are we waiting for?"

Nick needed no further invitation. Earlier he'd stuck a condom in his robe pocket. Now he fetched the wrapped package and tore it open. After encasing himself, he lifted her high in his arms and thrust deep within her.

Oh, the wonderful tightness of her. Could he ever get enough of Violet? Could she ever get enough of him? Not likely, it seemed, as she pulled him tighter into her, letting him push her into the wall. He supported her against the surface, letting her weight rest in his hands, feeling the warmth of her lips on his neck.

He set the pace this time, Violet moaning with every thrust. She tugged herself higher and widened her legs, taking him deeper.

It didn't take long. Violet's arms were firm around his neck, her cries muffled as she reached climax. When she did, she tightened, milking him, and he finished as well. Fast, but not furious, their lovemaking was a thing of opportunity and need.

The need to make love at every opportunity.

What a wonderful thing, to be with someone in this way. Most of his existence, Nick had been alone. Now he'd never be lonely again…he had Violet to be with.

To make love with. To grow old with. Violet to live his life with, and to experience her life as well. They'd never be alone, again. They had each other.

Nick leaned into the wall, supporting Violet in his arms. Life was perfect.

Or would be, as soon as he won his freedom.

Chapter Thirteen

Nick watched Violet's sleeping face, her breathing soft, stirring the hair that fell across her face. Gently he lifted the wayward lock and tucked it behind her ear. She was so beautiful, his woman, soon to be his wife. Beautiful. She slumbered deeply, tired from the long day, from the exercise he'd put her to.

He allowed himself a small smile. Violet was unaccustomed to making love several times a day but if he had his way, she'd soon grow used to it.

Not that he was used to such vigorous activity—but the goddess's gift of stamina had served him well these last two days. Even so, he was tired. Nick suppressed a yawn. What he wanted to do was collect Violet into his arms and fall asleep holding her. It was all he could do to say awake.

But his night wasn't over yet. He'd told Violet he'd be there in the morning, a man of flesh and blood, but he still needed to earn his freedom. He had to meet Nemesis…that is, Nina, in the park. Lifting his head, Nick read the glowing hands and numbers on the clock. Nearly one-thirty. He had half an hour to wait.

His stomach tightened. He wasn't looking forward to this meeting. The idea of sex with Nina felt…distasteful. Nick couldn't imagine how he'd manage to perform the same act with his enemy that he'd done with his beloved.

Making love with Violet was a joyous activity. When he was with her, he felt like a god.

With Nina, the best he could hope for was a quick end. He cared nothing for her or she for him. How could their coupling be anything but the act of two animals in rut?

Not that he had a choice. He was resigned to do what was needed to stay human.

But it still bothered him.

The minute hand crept closer to the hour. Nearly two-o'clock, time to go to the park. Wearily, Nick slipped from the bed and found his clothes, careful to not wake his sleeping lover. After tying his shoes, he paused in the doorway and took one last look at her face on the pillow. So lovely, sweet. He'd give anything to creep back into bed with her and spend the rest of the night holding her in his arms.

But if he were to have her to hold after tonight, he had to earn it. Grimly, Nick shut the door behind him.

As he entered the shadowy shed, he noted that the clean earthy odor of the place was overlaid with another smell, a perfume, musky and rich, almost cloying. The smell, so different from Violet's naturally clean scent, nearly turned his stomach. It reminded him of a flower, one of those that hunted living flesh for sustenance, using odor to attract and trap the unwary

It was Nina's smell. She waited in the shed for him like one of those flesh-eating plants, and he was the creature she hunted. The thought was almost enough to make him abandon his pursuit and return to Violet's bed.

But if he did, it would be only for a few hours, until the sun rose and he had to return to the park to resume his place as the statue by the fountain. Unless he earned his freedom, everything he wanted would be lost and Nina was the key to earning his freedom.

Even if he had to fuck her to do it.

Suppressing a sigh, Nick moved further inside, peering into the gloom, hoping to spot the woman. A laugh came from the shadows, the sound sharp as a knife, edged as much with anger as amusement.

"So, you did decide to come…I've been waiting for you." Moving out of the shadows, Nina slid into view. She wore a black gown that blended into the dark behind her, low-cut and sleeveless. Her bare arms and neck were pale against the fabric and as she reached for him, they appeared to come out of the dark at him, disembodied. He took a step backward, wary of her, and for the first time fear crept into him.

This was a very bad idea. He should give up and return to Violet. Maybe there was another way to earn the goddess's respect, short of intimacy with this creature.

She shook her black hair, and revealed her face, a shock of white in the darkness. "So quiet, Narcissus. Having second thoughts?"

"How do I know I'll be freed if I do this? You can't make this promise on your own."

Again her brittle laugh cut the quiet in the shed. "I thought you might think of that, so I got proof for you." Her pale hand reached out and he saw a parchment in it, the writing familiar even after three thousand years. Trembling, he took it, and opened it up, reading the Greek words emblazoned in gold.

I, Aphrodite, do swear that the bearer of this, Nemesis, does act in my behalf. Her word is the same as mine for the duration of this night.

Even the curling edges of the letters were the same as he'd seen the goddess use, hundreds of times while visiting her home during his disembodied time, before he'd become a statue.

It had to be genuine. Nemesis, that is Nina, wouldn't dare carry such a scroll without permission. Nick shivered again at what the penalty for such a transgression would be.

"So, Narcissus. Are you satisfied?" Nina stepped closer and he could see her more clearly, the bright gleam of anticipation in her eyes. She licked her lips, and without warning, Nick's cock reacted, hardening even as his stomach clenched in dismay. *Well, so much for not being able to perform.* Apparently the goddess's gift left him susceptible even to a woman he didn't really want.

Grimly he placed the scroll on the table. "Let's get to it," he told her, not bothering to cover the resignation in his voice.

Satisfaction in her face, Nina reached up and slid the narrow straps of her gown down off her shoulders. Nick's eyes widened at the sight of her bare torso, her breasts huge, the nipples puckered with excitement. His cock hardened to the point of pain and this time he couldn't stop his groan.

Nina smiled. "See, Nick. This isn't going to be so bad." Standing on her tiptoes, she draped her arms around his neck and slid her mouth across his. "This could turn out to be the best night of your life."

"I doubt it," he managed to say, then he crushed her to him, taking over her mouth with savage intensity, ignoring her amused chuckle.

* * * * *

The phone next to the bed was ringing, loud and insistent. Jarred from sleep, Violet grappled for the receiver with one hand, the other pulling her hair from her eyes as she took in the time on the clock. *Two-thirty?* What idiot would be calling her at this time of night?

"Violet, do you know where your boyfriend is?" Gary's voice was slurred, even more than it had been earlier, but she could still make out his words. He must have continued drinking after he left. He laughed, a nasty sound even through the phone.

Confused, Violet sat up, taking in the empty bed next to her. *Where was Nick?* "What have you done with him?" Concern turned her stomach into knots.

Gary's laugh grew wilder. "Me, nothing. I've just been watching, that's all. Your guy left the house and went to the park. I followed him there. He's in one of the sheds. Go look for yourself if you don't believe me." The phone went dead before she could say another word.

In the shed, the one they'd made love in? What was Nick doing there? Curiosity mixing with alarm, Violet dragged herself out of bed and found her clothes.

* * * * *

Nick dropped his head onto one of Nina's heavy breasts, nibbling the tip with practiced care. His fingers probed deep between Nina's thighs, using the skills he'd learned loving Violet to bring the nymph to a frenzied state. Under his hands, her full breasts quivered and she moaned loudly.

His cock throbbed, eager for more, even if he wasn't. All he could think about was how he wished it was Violet under him. He had to force himself to stay focused on sucking Nina's tit. She didn't even taste good to him, leaving a bitterness in his mouth. With difficulty, Nick tried to ignore Nina's fingernails digging into his back as he moved his fingers against her clit. He might have known the little wildcat would be all claws when engaged in sex.

She sunk her teeth into his shoulder and Nick stopped, jerking back. "Hey, that hurt! What are you trying to do, leave your mark on me?"

Nina didn't have the grace to look guilty. She grinned, her pointed little teeth looking ready to take another bite out of him. "Can I help it if you drive me wild, lover?"

"Don't call me that," he growled.

"Why not...*lover*. That's what you are, you know. And what are you afraid of, anyway...that your 'sweetheart' will find out what you've been up to?"

"Leave Violet out of this. This is between you and me, Nina, and it's only to get me free. After this I never want to see you again."

"Really," she purred. "Well then, you better get back to work. I'm not finished yet and until I'm satisfied, you aren't free of anything."

Lowering his head, Nick began again. If the little slut wanted satisfaction, he'd give it to her. She scratched harder and he bit down on the nipple, hoping to make her stop.

"Oh, yes, Nick..." she babbled. "Like that—yes, harder."

Might have known she'd like that, he grumbled to himself. Engrossed, he completely missed the sound of the shed door creak open.

"Nick?"

It was the pain in Violet's voice that he noticed. Pulling away from Nina, he twisted on the floor, gazing into Violet's horrified face. His own horror rose as her stare took in him, Nina behind him, their nakedness, his hard cock bobbing in front of him.

Merciful gods! He held up his hand to her. "It isn't what you think, Violet."

A short bark of a laugh escaped her. "Oh really? Then what is it? It looks like you're having sex with another woman."

His heart sank to his toes, his cock shriveling under her withering stare. "Yes, but there's a reason."

"Of course there is. There always is." She shuddered, a sob breaking free. "I might have known you'd be like any other man. If it's warm and willing, why not screw it."

"I didn't want to..."

"Oh, I'm sure." Another choked-off laugh erupted from her. "I can see how you've been forced into this, just like you were forced to ask me to be your wife. Well, that's one thing I can remedy." She struggled with her hand, pulled the ring from her finger. With surprisingly strong arm, she flung it at him, hitting him in the chest. Nick clutched at it but it slipped through his fingers to the floor. "I never want to see you again."

Storming from the shed, she left the door ajar. Nick was after her in a moment, the cold air outside reminding him of his state of undress. He caught up with her halfway down the path. Violet struck at him, her fists flailing as he pulled her to the covering darkness under one of the trees.

"If you don't let go of me, I'll scream."

"No, please. Listen to me." He held her tight, taking the blows, the pain far less than what was already in his heart. He buried his head in her hair. "Please, Violet. It was for us, I swear it. The price of my freedom."

She stopped her wild hitting and collapsed into his arms, her tears hot against his bare chest. "The price? To become free, you had to make love with another woman?"

"Nina was the woman who originally cursed me. She was the nymph I rejected, although she was called Nemesis then. She got Aphrodite to agree to release me, but the price was…what you saw. It wasn't lovemaking, Violet. Never that. I don't care for her, not at all. I love only you."

She raised her tearstained face to his. "Why didn't you tell me, then? You let me believe you'd already been released."

"I didn't want you to know. I didn't want you to be hurt."

Another short barking laugh came out of her. "Too late for that, Nick. I am hurt. Seeing you with her…" her voice broke off, choked by sobs. She pushed her way out of his arms. "No matter how bad it was with Gary or any other man I've known, I've never felt like this before. I trusted you. Too quickly, I can see. You aren't that different from the others…when it's convenient you'll lie and sneak around. You didn't trust me enough to tell me the truth."

The truth of her words hit harder than her fists had. Nick released her and watched her step away.

For a moment neither of them spoke. What could he say to her? That fucking Nina hadn't meant anything to him? That wasn't the point…it had meant something to Violet, no matter what he'd thought about it. The tears on her face were proof of that. "I'm sorry, Violet."

She glanced at the shed. "I guess you weren't quite finished. You should get back."

The last thing he wanted was to return to Nina, but she had a point. He'd been close to satisfying the woman when they'd been discovered. "Violet, will I find you at home?"

She nodded briefly, not meeting his eyes. "I'll be there." She took off for the edge of the park, her stride fast.

Nick leaned against the tree, feeling the rough bark abrade his skin. Here and there sharp pain from the scratches Nina had inflicted on him reminded him of his dilemma…not that he needed reminding. The truth burning into his soul was sufficient.

Nick had wanted to show Violet how deserving of love she was by giving her his. He'd asked her to spend her life with him, then, within hours had hurt her worse than anyone else could have. She'd given him unconditional trust, only to have him violate it.

He'd thought he could be the best man for her.

He wasn't.

Nick felt the sting of his scratches and let them tell him the truth. Centuries ago he'd been punished for his self-centered nature, and all he'd proven since becoming flesh was that he hadn't changed a bit. It had been his own interests he'd been pursuing with Violet. He'd wanted her to be his woman, for his sake, not for hers. He hadn't thought to consider there might be someone better for her.

Someone more deserving.

Someone who'd never hurt her.

Someone who wasn't him.

Violet deserved a man who would never hurt her, and that man was clearly not himself. Nick didn't deserve her. He never would, no matter how much he wanted it.

Nick pushed open the door to the shed to see Nina still sitting on the floor, her lips twisted into a wicked smile. Nick gazed at her, noting her perfect features. She really was beautiful to the eye, but inside she was mean spirited and ugly.

She held out her arms to him. "So, lover boy, you ready to begin again? You were doing good until your girlfriend showed up. Really had me going."

A flash of silver near his feet caught his eye…the ring he'd given Violet when he'd asked her to be his wife. Nick's heart shattered at the sight. Bending, he picked it up, held it in the dim light, and brushed off the dirt that clung to the delicate flowers engraved on the band. Slipping it onto his smallest finger, he stepped around Nina to collect his clothes.

She watched him, consternation in her gaze. "What are you doing?"

"Leaving. Going…" he caught himself. He'd almost said he was going home, but Violet's house would never be his home now. "I'm going back to Violet's."

"But we aren't done. You haven't earned your freedom."

Pulling on his pants, he fastened them at the waist. Clever things zippers, once you got practiced with them. It was a shame he'd not be able to take advantage of his expertise in the future. "It doesn't matter now, Nina. I only wanted my freedom so I could be with Violet. That's not going to happen now."

She pouted, a pretty maneuver that most likely would usually bring a man to his knees. Nick felt his gut twist instead.

"You don't know that," she told him. "Maybe your flower will change her mind and take you back once you're human for good. If you leave now you go back to being a statue for all time. Is that what you want?"

"It doesn't matter what I want. It never did, really." Nick sighed as he finished tying his shoes. "I only wanted what was best for her. I thought that was me, but it wasn't."

Nina's dark eyed gaze turned thoughtful. "You really love her, don't you?"

Stopping by the door, Nick nodded, slowly. "Yeah, I do." Straightening his shoulders, he stepped outside into the night air. "See you 'round the park, Nina."

Chapter Fourteen

Nick let himself into the house using Gary's key. He'd taken it earlier before leaving, hoping to avoid Violet's notice when he'd returned from his liaison with Nina…not that there was any point to the subterfuge any more.

The clock on the wall read three-twenty. Three hours until sunrise, when he would have to return to his pedestal and take up his non-life as a garden decoration once more. Having left Nina unsatisfied, he had no hopes of avoiding that fate.

He almost looked forward to solidifying and not feeling anything anymore. It would be a relief to put this human condition aside again and have nothing more serious than the condition of the birdbath at his feet to worry about.

Almost. If it weren't for missing Violet, he'd look forward to being a statue again. But Violet was a part of his life now, such as it was. He'd miss her when he left this mortal state.

He'd miss her terribly.

Closing the door behind him, Nick put the key on the table nearby. When he left at dawn, he'd leave it behind. It wasn't like he would need it again.

He wouldn't be back.

After a moment's hesitation, he also pulled off Violet's ring and put it near the key. He'd thought to take it with him, to remember her. But he didn't need anything to remind him of Violet.

Violet wasn't in the living room or the front part of the house. He checked out the bathroom, but she wasn't there either. The door to her bedroom was closed. Nick hesitated a moment, but then opened it up.

The room was dark, much as it had been when he'd left it. Violet was on the bed, a small lump under the blanket, and for a moment he thought she was asleep.

"So…are you free?"

She was calmer now. He could hear it in her voice, but he could also hear unforgiveness as well.

"No." The one word was all he could say.

She shifted, sat up. Through the window came moonlight, soft and pale. Through it Nick could make out her confused features.

"No? I don't understand."

"No—I didn't finish. I couldn't. I didn't want to." He stammered out an answer for her. "I never wanted Nemesis in the first place. I only tried to give her what she wanted because it was the only way I could stay with you. But the price was too high. If I did what she wanted, I hurt you and lost you, and without you humanity wasn't worth having. It wasn't worth it," he finished.

She was silent a long time. "You gave up your chance to stay human? Just to avoid hurting me?"

He angered at the disbelief in her voice. "I told you I love you. How could I do anything deliberately to cause you pain? If you believe nothing else about me, know that, Violet."

"I do believe you." Her voice had a catch in it. "Tomorrow..."

Nick sat on the bed. "Tomorrow morning I have to return to the park. Aphrodite will meet me there and make me into a statue again."

She turned her face to him, her blue eyes large with sorrow and unshed tears. "You really need to go back? Because of me?"

How could he explain this to her? "It's not your fault, Violet. I'm the one who upset the goddess, centuries ago. She gave me a chance to atone, but I wasn't willing to pay the price. You were right, that I didn't deserve you."

"I never said that...I never believed that. I couldn't believe you wanted me, and when I saw you with someone else, I couldn't stand it. Now you have to go back and it's all my fault!"

Nick moved closer, until she was just within his reach. "No, Violet, it was my choice. I did want you. I still do. But I was wrong to think I was the best man for you. You deserve better than me, Violet. You deserve someone you can be proud of, not a minor mythical character, someone whose very name means self-absorbed." He took a deep breath. "You deserve a hero, Violet. Not me."

Violet reached for him, taking his hand in hers. "I don't want a hero, Nick. I want a friend, a lover. And that's you."

Nick raised her hand to his lips. "We can still be friends, Violet. I'll wait by the pool, and you'll come and talk to me. If you listen real hard, you'll be able to hear me. I'll try to speak to you."

"No!" Her impassioned cry broke his heart. Nick pulled her into his arms and held her as she cried.

Stroking her hair, he murmured. "I will always love you, Violet."

He held her until her tears were gone and, exhausted physically and mentally, she drifted off to sleep.

* * * * *

Nick was gone from the bed when she woke, the sky still dark on the horizon. Panicked, Violet threw off the covers and ran from the bedroom. In the living room and bathroom, there was no sign of him. His clothes still hung in the closet and only the garment he'd been wearing when she'd met him in the park was gone.

There couldn't be more than a half-hour before dawn, when Nick would return to his old state—become a statue again. Quickly Violet threw her clothes on, a flowered sweatshirt and jeans from her closet. She pulled on her shoes and headed for the front door. Then she saw the ring he'd given her, sitting by a house key on the table. She snatched it up and the key, using it to lock the door on the way out.

He'd be in the park. She had to catch up to him, had to at least say goodbye. All the love they'd known during the past two nights...she couldn't let him go without telling him. She hadn't said it, not really. With all of the words spoken, all the passionate phrases of the last few hours...

She hadn't said the simplest one, the one with the least words that meant the most.

She hadn't said, "I love you."

* * * * *

The park was deserted and for a moment Violet wondered if she was too late, but then she saw the empty fountain pedestal. Across from it was the park bench where she'd first met Nick, and there he was, sitting, waiting. As she came up, his despondent body jerked erect, and he smiled.

Breathing hard, Violet came to an abrupt stop in front of him. "You didn't wake me up. You left without saying goodbye."

The smile fled and pain filled his eyes at the hurt in her voice. "I know. I'm sorry. I thought it best..." His words stopped and started, and he looked everywhere but at her. "I didn't want you to see me go. I thought it best you remember me as I am now, not...not as cold stone."

Her hand grabbed his, pulled it to her lips. "I will remember you always, Nick, regardless of whether or not I saw you leave. But I want to be here to say goodbye."

A breeze picked up and the sky lightened a little. Nick startled and looked around him. "You should go—no telling what mood Aphrodite will be in this early in the morning. Goddesses aren't good to be around when they're cranky."

"No, I want to stay. Please, Nick, I want to spend all the time I can with you." She settled onto the bench next to him. "Please don't make me go."

Now he looked at her and she could see the love in his brown eyes. "I couldn't make you leave me. Never." He brushed a lock of hair from her face. "If I could, I'd be with you forever."

She pulled the ring from her pocket and put it on her finger again. "I'd stay with you forever, too, Nick."

They kissed and time disappeared in the swell of soft words and loving touches. They were still in each other's arms when a whirlwind developed unnoticed by the empty pedestal. Once more leaves, dirt, and flower blossoms created the shape of a woman, and when the dust settled down, the goddess stood once more in the garden.

She gazed at the pair on the bench, oblivious to her presence, and tapped one golden sandal impatiently. "So, Narcissus, have you learned what you wanted to know?"

At her voice, Violet and Nick startled apart, both turning to face the impassive face of the goddess. Violet stared. Aphrodite was gloriously beautiful, but as Nick had warned her, she did seem out of sorts, as if she wasn't used to being up so early in the morning.

"I learned what I could, Glorious One." Nick said, his voice cautious.

"Did you?" One perfect eyebrow rose slightly as she turned to gaze at Violet. "Were you disappointed in your selection of a teacher?"

"No, not at all." Nick spoke quickly, his eyes wide in concern. "Violet was wonderful…"

"Then what do you mean? Speak, I don't have all day."

Nick placed his arm around Violet's shoulders and pulled her closer. "What I mean is that there is far more to love than attraction and sex, Magnificent Lady. I mean that true love is sharing more than a few hours…wonderful as those hours were. I wanted to spend the rest of my life with her."

"Did you? You would give up immortality to live with a human?" She didn't look like she believed Nick.

"I would have."

"And yet, when given the opportunity to earn your freedom, you refused my nymph again." The goddess shook her golden head. "You have no idea how provoked she was."

"Mighty One..." Nick spoke hesitantly. "If I had done as she'd asked...passed Nemesis's test and satisfied her, would I have stayed human?"

"Of course. You don't think I make empty promises. But if you had, you would have lost your lady. Right Violet?"

At being addressed directly, Violet started. Then she noticed the glint of sympathy in the goddess's eye. "I—I don't know. I might have forgiven him."

"No, you wouldn't have. Not really," Aphrodite said gently. "Some sins can never be absolved, unfaithfulness being the most common. Think about all the trouble Zeus has had with Hera, and all because he can't keep his tunic on. I swear it's enough to give me a complex."

The goddess frowned. "They always blame me, you know. 'Just couldn't help themselves', 'lust blinded them'." She shook her head in disgust. "You'd think I invented sex and not merely embodied it. Trust me, sex has been around a lot longer than I have."

"Sex is wonderful," Nick assured her. "With the right person, it's making love and making love is amazing. I will always treasure the memory of it. I only wish..."

Both perfect eyebrows rose in unison. "Another wish?"

Quickly Nick shook his head. "No, no further wishes, Great One. I must be satisfied with what I have."

Aphrodite clapped her hands and gave them a brief smile. "Very well then. I'm glad you're satisfied. Dawn is coming and we must put you back. Say goodbye to your mortal friend and get back on the pedestal."

He faced Violet and gently stroked her face. The tears that had threatened finally flooded her eyes and she couldn't help one brief sob. "Nick..."

Nick wiped her tears away, then gently kissed her lips, soft and sweet. "No tears, my love. What we've had cannot be taken from us, so long as we remember. Come visit me, Violet. Come and tell me your news as you used to." He smiled. "We can still be friends, you and I."

Then he pulled away and strode quickly to the fountain, climbed up and crouched by the pool of water. On the horizon the light grew and any second now the edge of the sun would peek over and dawn would arrive. Nick stilled, taking the position the sculptor had given him so long ago, gazing into the pool at his own reflection. "I'm ready, Aphrodite."

The edge of the sun appeared, and Nick's feet turned pale. Violet watched the tan flesh of his ankles harden.

"NO, WAIT!" At her cry Nick's head turned to her and she saw the pain, the want in his face.

"Violet." It was the only word he said, the last one he would speak, but all of his love was in it.

She dashed to the pedestal and climbed up, just as the sun rose into the sky. On hands and knees she moved along the edge of the pool until her face was inches from his. "Nick, I love you."

It was all she spoke. When the sunlight hit the fountain, she was still there, turned to white marble.

Chapter Fifteen

"Hey look, Edgar, the statue has a girlfriend now."

Edgar leaned back, pushed his baseball cap further up his head, and stared at the altered fountain group. Sure enough, another figure had been added. A woman on hands and knees perched next to Narcissus, her face tilted toward his. The male statue's face was inches from hers, his lips pursed as if to meet hers in a kiss, one marble hand poised to caress the back of her head. It looked like the pair had been close to a full-on lip-lock when interrupted.

"Well if that don't beat all," he said. "Must be those art types again, foolin' around." He got up to examine the woman more closely, and laughed. "Yeah, it's got to be a joke. Look, she's wearing jeans, you can see the label!"

Both men had a good laugh and went on to finish their work. As soon as they were gone, a little whirlwind formed and an amused voice spoke. "I knew I'd forgotten something."

Immediately the marble clothing melted away, leaving only the naked form of a woman on her hands and knees next to the pool. The unseen voice chuckled. "My name, little Violet, is Aphrodite. You might want to practice it…there may be a test.

The new fountain group caught considerable attention all day. Several men and women from the city museum came by and admired the workmanship. Even the marble was as good as that of the original statue.

"I think she's fat." That was from a young girl with a thin frame, breasts barely pushing out the front of her top.

"Naw, that's the way she's supposed to look," stated the young man with her. "All those old Greek nymphs were chubby." He eyed the statue with a lecherous grin. "Her boobs sure are big."

He was sorry when his girlfriend refused to talk to him for the rest of the day.

Mothers of young children made a point to keep their offspring away from the fountain. The half-naked young man had been bad enough, but this new figure left nothing to the imagination. Several commented that they were going to complain to the park authorities as soon as they got home.

Two young men took particular notice of the woman statue's position, her rear being just the right height for a little doggie-style action. Too bad the male statue was on the wrong side, they sniggered.

Evening fell and the park became quiet and deserted, and once more an inaudible chant began, a male voice speaking in modern English:

"Oh mighty Aphrodite, Goddess of Beauty,

Get back here you infernal Bitch!"

In a whirl of breeze and leaves, Aphrodite appeared, a glass of white wine in hand, her face in an amused smirk. She laughed, clearly pleased with herself.

"Is something wrong, Narcissus?" she asked in her crystalline voice.

Nick's voice seethed. "How could you do this, turn her to stone? Why? Violet did nothing wrong, she doesn't deserve this."

Aphrodite studied the statue that used to be Violet Smith. "I don't see what you're complaining about, Narcissus. I gave you what you wanted. You said you wanted her, and I gave her to you, even provided you with a view of her face, something you said you desired above all things. Remember I told you I'd be listening. I've gone well beyond our bargain to please you."

There was a strain in Nick's voice, as he wrestled with his temper. "I'm sure you understand that I would never have wanted Violet to become a statue, Mighty One."

"Why not? You've enjoyed being one all these years. Maybe she does, too?" The goddess tapped Violet's shoulder with one delicate finger. "Tell him, Violet. Isn't this what you wanted, wasn't this your secret wish?"

Violet's voice was weak and unsure, as if she didn't quite know how to speak. "I…I…"

"That's fine, dear." Aphrodite coaxed. "I know it's difficult at first, but you'll get the hang of it. Just think the answer, really hard."

"I…" Violet tried again. "I…wanted…to be with…Narcissus!" she finished triumphantly.

"No!" Nick answered, horrified. "This was your secret wish, to become a statue?"

"Well, no." Violet admitted. "I didn't want to be like this, cold and stiff, unable to feel, taste, or smell." Her voice turned pleading. "I just wanted to be with you, any way I could."

"And I want to be with you, but we can't do it this way. Take back the wish, Violet. Ask to be human again."

Her voice turned stubborn, and he realized that Violet was no longer the meek, mild-mannered woman he'd met. "No, Nick. It was my decision and I made it. I don't want to live without you. I love you too much."

"I love you, too. But I can't let you throw your life away for me. How selfish would that make me, to have you here with me, but at the cost of your freedom?" His voice broke. "I love you, Violet, but imagine what torture this is for me. Your hair close to my hand, your lips raised to mine. So close to me, but just beyond reach. If we could move, we'd touch, but we can't move. I can't stand this, Violet."

"I know it's a torture for me, too, but…"

"Is that all that's wrong?" Aphrodite's voice chirped up, brightly. "You wish to touch and that will make this better?" She clapped her hands. "That's easy enough to fix."

She placed her hands on their necks, and the stone softened. Nick and Violet's heads moved together into a completion of their kiss, the marble making a grinding sound as their stone lips met.

The grinding sound stopped when the marble lost it pallor and became the color and texture of flesh. First the lips, then the cheeks and noses, then it continued down their necks and to the rest of their bodies. Nick's hand descended onto the back of Violet's head, hitting soft hair and not sculpted curls. Swiftly the change continued until Violet and Nick both were returned to the shape of mortal man and woman.

Nick broke off their kiss and leaned back, staring into Violet's smiling blue eyes. He turned to Aphrodite, watching with a bemused expression. "What is this?" He held up his hand, flexed his fingers. "I'm alive again."

"Indeed, you are. It seems you have passed the final test, Narcissus, the real one. Even when given your heart's desire, to be with your lady at her own request, you could not be selfish. You are free now, to remain a mortal human being if that's what you desire."

His face lit with astonishment and he stared at Violet, leaning back on her heels. "Violet. We can be together."

Joy filled her and she leapt into his arms and kissed him. "We can be together, Nick, for all time. I love you."

He clutched her closer. "I love you, too."

A cool breeze came up and Violet shivered. "I don't suppose you could return my clothes now," she asked the goddess. "Please, Aphrodite?"

Aphrodite smiled. "You finally got my name correct." She pursed her lips and nodded briefly. "I think the pair of you look lovely as you are, but I suppose it is a bit cold." She waved one delicate hand and Nick and Violet were once more dressed in jeans and sweatshirts, jogging shoes on their feet. When she checked, Violet found her house key in her pocket.

"Now run along home, you two, and live happily ever after."

They climbed off the fountain and headed past the bench. Aphrodite listened to their excited chatter.

"Nick, about what those guys said."

"About you being chubby." He hugged her close. "You're just the way a woman should look."

She blushed prettily. "Thanks, but I meant about my position when I was on the pedestal…remember how much fun we had doing it that way?"

Nick grinned. "Oh, that. Yeah, I was thinking the same thing. Let's run home and see if it's as good."

The pair sped down the garden path.

The goddess smiled. Turning to the now empty fountain, she thought for a moment. "Hmm…we need a replacement." With a wave of her hand, a new statue stood in place posed as Narcissus had been, and fearlessly naked. Remembering what the park mothers had complained about, she sketched one hand and a simple shepherd's garment now decorated the waist, covering the man's privates.

The man now staring into the pool resembled Gary, Violet's ex-boyfriend, his face caught in an expression of surprise.

"Yes, that will do for now." Aphrodite said in quiet satisfaction. She tapped the new statue on the shoulder. "Maybe someday you'll look beyond your own desires and see someone to love. In the meantime, enjoy the view."

A swirl of wind, and the goddess disappeared.

Epilogue

"And in conclusion, it is clear from the evidence that stonemasons from Iona were instrumental in the creation of the temples of Athens." Nick checked the last sentence for grammar and spelling errors, and then saved the file, nodding satisfaction. *It was done, finally.* He burned the final version of his thesis onto a CD before shutting down his new shiny white laptop.

Done, the last hurdle to his degree, the one thing he needed to keep his teaching position at the university, academic recognition of his expertise of the ancient world. When he and Violet had arrived home a year ago tonight, freed from the curse, they'd found an envelope with all kinds of useful documentation, including a social security card, birth certificate, and school records, all in the name of Nicholas Rockman.

Just another of the Goddess's little jokes.

He'd taken a few months to get up to speed in reading and writing English, and then had applied to the university as a graduate student. His knowledge of ancient Greece and Rome had caught the professors' attention and soon the anthropology department had put him on the staff as an assistant, subject to his finishing his thesis. Now the position would be permanent.

Nick smiled at the accomplishment. From lawn ornament to scholar in a single year…not bad for a three-thousand-year-old man! With his salary, Violet would have to work much less in the future and he'd be able to take care of their expenses.

From the living room, Violet's tuneless humming broke through his thoughts. Taking the disk with him, Nick left the office nook in their bedroom and, as he'd expected, found her in the bentwood rocker she loved so much. He grinned. It had been a stroke of genius to figure out when Gary's new landlady would get fed up with her absentee tenant and sell off his property. He'd made a point of getting to her garage sale first, buying all the items Violet's former boyfriend had taken.

She'd been delighted to see her belongings again, only wasting a few moments wondering what had happened to the odious man. Funny thing—she'd noticed the new statue in the garden but hadn't figured out whom Aphrodite had chosen to take Nick's place.

Nick had recognized Gary at once. He knew the goddess and how much she loved a joke, almost as much as she loved a good love story. Watching Violet, rocking gently in her chair, he was glad to be part of the latter and not the former.

She glanced up and her smile welcomed his approach. "You finished?"

He held up the disk. "Just now. Two hundred pages on Grecian columns, ready for publication."

"Wonderful, Nick!" Even after a year, Violet's praise still warmed him like no other's. Making her proud had become one of the most important parts of his life.

"How's your project coming?" He pointed to the elongated square dangling from the long knitting needles. "Isn't that a little big?"

She lifted the work and examined it ruefully. "It was supposed to be booties, then a sweater. Now I think I'm making an afghan."

"Well, any of the three would keep our baby warm." Nick pulled her from the chair and cuddled her close, his hand stroking the five-month bulge under the robe. "I see you've taken to wearing mine."

"Mine barely fits around my middle," Violet complained, her lips finding his chin. "Yours is much more comfortable," she told him as she nibbled.

Slipping his hand inside the robe, he found the tightened flesh that covered his child. It was still a little soon for him to consistently feel the baby's movements, but knowing he or she was there, resting in Violet's body, sent a thrill shooting through him.

His child in his wife, his seed come to life, just as he'd wished for a year ago. Life was wonderful.

Stroking her bare belly, he discovered that it wasn't the only thing bare about her. The soft curls of her woman's mound tickled his fingers when he dipped past the slight bulge.

"You aren't wearing any underwear," he said, pulling the robe further open, reveling in the sight. No bra, no panties, just Violet, gloriously pregnant. As full-chested as she had been, now her breasts were magnificent things. Nick's mouth watered.

She glowed under his heated gaze, and not because of the baby. Desire lit her face and she reached to tug free the bottom of his shirt. "I was thinking we should celebrate."

"Celebrate is good. You can't have any champagne, though," he told her through gritted teeth as she opened his shirt and stroked the new hair that had grown across his chest in the past year.

"And chocolate isn't good. I've already gained six pounds this month." She leaned over and licked his nipples. Nick forced back a groan. "What we need is something that has no calories, or alcohol. Hmm…What would you suggest?"

Oh how he loved this second trimester horniness. Since Violet had stopped feeling ill, at the end of the first three months, she'd been persistently pulling his clothes off at odd moments of the day, demanding he satisfy her hormone-driven body. It was enough to make Nick wonder how many children they could have. One experience with pregnancy wasn't going to be enough.

Of course, her hormones were only part of it. Bold little Violet she'd become since their first meeting, no longer uncertain of who she was, but now a woman who knew her own mind and what she wanted from life.

Nick thanked all the gods that what she wanted was him in her as often as possible.

Pulling the robe off her, he placed it over the chair behind her to cushion her as he directed her back into the seat. Violet leaned against the back as he knelt before her and spread her legs wide over the rocking chair arms. Nick took a moment to admire the sight of her opened folds before leaning in to taste her. She squirmed and moaned as he tongued the hardened nub of her clit, reveling in the tangy juices already pooling from her slit.

Violet's hands dug into his hair, urging him onward. Nick reached behind her to grasp the back of the chair, supporting her between his arms and moving the chair to and fro. The gentle rocking made it easier to set his pace.

The rocking gave him other ideas, too.

Violet shuddered under his ministrations, her clit throbbing under his tongue, her hands clenching at his head in unleashed passion. "Come for me," he whispered.

She did, crying out his name. Nick stood and caught her as she collapsed forward into his arms. Easing her back into the chair, he turned her so she knelt on the seat cushion and could rest her arms against the back.

His pants came off in one movement, his mind so full of the sight of her rounded buttocks that it barely registered he should have removed his shoes first. After a little struggle he was naked, thinking Violet's post-climax euphoria had hidden his clumsiness.

Her grin as he approached told him she hadn't missed a thing. "Nice to know I can still fluster you, my husband, even in my current bulging state."

"You are the most beautiful woman alive, Violet," he chided her. "And you know it, too. Look what you do to me." He watched her eyes widen at the sight of his cock, massive and ready for her. He gave it a couple of preliminary pulls, spreading the pre-cum along the shaft, enjoying the feel of his hand, knowing how good the feel of her pussy was going to be.

She started to climb off the chair, but he stopped her. "Lean forward against the chair, Violet."

Anticipation in her pose, she did, lifting her ass obediently in the air. He found her woman's opening from behind and slipped partway inside. Her welcoming sigh told him she was prepared for this and he slid home within her tight, enclosing warmth.

He breathed deeply, reaching for control. She felt wonderful and he wanted this to last. Violet shot a glance over her shoulder, her eyes bright with pleasure. Nick pulled up on the arms of the chair and it rocked back, taking her with it. His cock slid slowly out of her. When he pushed down on the arms, she slid back onto his shaft. He repeated the action, and Violet rocked with the chair, his cock sliding in and out with the movement of the chair.

Violet rocked and moaned, Nick's hips taking up the action as well. He thrust deep within her, using the arms of the chair to keep Violet in movement.

Deeper he plunged, harder than he'd dared in recent months. The doctor had assured him sex wouldn't hurt Violet or the baby, but still he'd been hesitant. Now hesitation left him. Nick reached forward to caress his woman's full, heavy breasts, the round belly where his child lay, and he let his body speak to her of everything in his heart.

She was his to possess, his to love, to take care of, to protect. His woman, carrying his child, the pair of them his family. Emotions of love crowded those of desire and still he thrust deeply into her glorious body, letting this possession of her stand as a symbol for what he felt.

She was his Violet, in the roses, in the bedroom, or in any other place he could hold her and love her. He would care for her—as a woman, as a wife—and support her as she supported him, mentally and physically.

She was his Violet, forever.

The End

ECHO IN THE HALL

Cricket Starr

Preview

The second in the Divine Interventions series by Cricket Starr, available July 2004.

Chapter One

She came alive at midnight.

Alex crept down the darkened museum hallway and ducked behind one of the tall Grecian urns that flanked the opening to the adjacent gallery. From his hiding place he peered at the statue standing in the middle of the gallery. It was a beautiful thing, a slender stone figure of a woman just visible behind the marble representation of a tree. At the foot of the tree was a plaque: *Echo, A Greek Nymph.*

The face of the statue was frozen into a visage of longing and unrequited desire so poignant that when he'd first seen it, he'd thought her face the most beautiful in the world.

At least that's what he'd thought until several weeks ago when he worked late on a Thursday night and inadvertently discovered her true beauty.

The change in the statue started just as he heard the great clock in the museum lobby begin to chime twelve. At first it was subtle, just a hint of color to the white marble of the nymph's body, but then the color darkened and spread across the stone as if a film had been laid over it. Long curls of hair decorating her head and hanging down her back darkened to pale gold, while rosy hues made pink her fingers and bare toes. A deep blush stole across the statue's cheeks as her lips deepened to the most enticing red.

For an instant the statue seemed alive as her eyelids blinked over irises now green instead of white, but then the film of color lifted away from the stone to form a ghostly outline of a woman, misty and indistinct. The ghost stepped back, leaving the statue as it had been—cold, unliving stone. As Alex watched, her transparency disappeared and she grew more solid, a spirit made beautiful flesh.

The first time he'd seen her come alive, he'd panicked, convinced he was seeing a ghost. Only the fact that he didn't carry a weapon had kept him from pumping lead into her—or more likely through her and into the museum wall. Thank goodness he hadn't done something that stupid. He'd certainly have had a problem explaining that to the museum's manager.

Without a gun, he'd remained frozen in place behind the stone urns until the ethereal figure had returned to the gallery to meld back into the statue, leaving no sign that she'd been there at all. When she'd repeated the process the following week, Alex had summoned the courage to follow her, this time noticing how tentative her movements were and how careful she was to avoid notice. She was more afraid than he was.

Alex grinned to himself. He'd found out what was pulling her out of her hiding place, why she was coming alive. By the third week, he was looking forward to her visit, watching her every move with fascination. Guarding an empty museum was usually pretty boring. With Echo coming to life, things had gotten more interesting.

This was the fourth week and he'd decided it was time for them to meet.

Alex wished he had his camera with him so he could capture her beauty for all time. Echo would make a marvelous model, he'd stake his growing reputation as a student photographer on it. As her body solidified, the simple white, off-the-shoulder gown she wore stayed sheer, revealing rose-tipped nipples and the inviting thatch of golden curls that covered her woman's mound.

Alex's cock hardened at the same time she did, and for once he was grateful for the looseness of his second-hand security guard's uniform. The job was temporary so rather than spend the money for a new one he'd made due with a cast-off from the previous guard, a much larger man.

Pants that fit well would be very uncomfortable in his aroused state. Even so, it was hard not to groan aloud when she stretched her hands over her head and those heavy breasts lifted into full relief against their fabric covering.

Echo swung about in his direction, her dangly earrings making a soft tinkling in the quiet of the museum. Alex wondered if he'd made a noise, and froze in place, holding his breath. If she heard him, she'd flee back into the statue and he'd miss his chance tonight. She only came out on Thursdays at midnight, and even then only for this one specific purpose. Alex bit down on his lip.

Her great green eyes searched the darkness of the gallery, tension in her stance. For a moment Alex thought she would give up and flee, but then a woman's throaty laugh came from another part of the museum. Echo turned in that direction, and longing replaced her watchful caution. She took a few hesitant steps then sped down the corridor in the direction the laugh had come from.

Moving as quietly as he could, Alex followed.

When he caught up with her, she was outside the entrance to the museum offices, her ear against the closed door. Alex heard another laugh, deep and male. Echo straightened and waved her hand and the door before her wavered, then appeared to fade away. Inside the now-revealed room, the occupants continued to talk and laugh, apparently unaware that they were exposed to Echo's rapt stare.

Alex took up a position behind the large urn across the hall. From his vantage point he could watch her and the couple inside the room.

"Nick, we've got to stop meeting like this." The museum's assistant curator, Violet Smith Rockman, ran her hand down the shirtfront of the tall handsome man standing next to her. "Someone's going to hear us."

Nicholas Rockman, associate professor of antiquities at the nearby city college, collected her hand and kissed it. "Since our daughter was born, the museum is the one place we can make as much noise as we want. You work late on Thursday night…this is the only time we do this, when no one is around."

Violet used her free hand to tug Nick's shirt out of his pants. "But the security guard…"

"…is way on the other side of the building." Nick slipped his hands under Violet's sweater, fondling the heavy breasts underneath. "We have twenty minutes before he gets back here."

"Twenty minutes…that's not much time." Violet's busy fingers sped along the buttons of Nick's shirt, revealing his lightly haired chest. She leaned over and licked his nipples, and Nick let loose a low groan.

Near the door, Echo put her hand over her mouth, suppressing her own groan.

"I know, but we still have enough time for this." Nick pulled Violet's sweater off,and unfastened her bra.

As fascinated he was with Echo, Alex couldn't help but admire Violet's naked breasts. He knew she was breastfeeding but even so, they were enormous. Envy slashed through him as Nick kneaded the luscious globes and licked her swollen nipples.

Alex did his best to suppress a groan. He loved the feel of a plump nipple between his lips. One problem with his self-imposed celibacy was not having a woman's tits to suck.

Not that he'd really had a choice after Mel-the-Bitch had dumped him. His former girlfriend had taken exception to his leaving the lucrative business of marketing and applying to graduate school to study photography. Melody had been fine with his obsession of taking photos in his spare time, in the limited moments of the evening and the occasional weekend hours. She'd been too busy with her own concerns, spending time with her friends, trips to the shopping mall, manicures, and visits to the local spa.

Melody Martin had had any number of ways to spend her time—and his money—in entertaining herself.

But then he'd given up his soul-sucking job and announced that he was going back to school to study photography full time. It was his dream to become a professional photographer. The local university had classes he could take, but they were only offered during the day. He'd taken the security job at the museum to cover basic expenses so they'd have to scrimp for a while.

Once through school he could become a professional and earn a healthy income from doing what he loved best.

It would only take a little time, he'd told Mel.

Too much time, apparently. Melody had taken a single day to try and "talk sense" to him, and when she'd failed to change his mind had packed her bags and much of their apartment and left, cleaning out their joint bank account at the same time. She'd even taken the kitchenware they'd picked out and he'd paid for, leaving his cupboards as empty as his bed.

Alex grimaced over that. He could forgive the money, but eating on cheap plastic plates with mismatched silverware got to a man. He'd gained ten pounds in the past year, a tribute to a steady diet of pizza and other fast food washed down with too much beer. Mel's defection had left him with little appetite for anything else, including women of any kind.

Celibacy was easier than dealing someone who would cut your heart out when you were least expecting it, even if you had to give up sucking on plump nipples for a while.

Until he'd seen Echo he'd been relatively content with that situation. Now he watched her and desire sped through him, reminding him how nice being with a woman could be. Tonight he'd at least try for a taste of what he'd been missing.

By the door, Echo's eyes darkened with passion as she watched the couple making love. When Nick licked Violet's nipples, Echo licked her own fingers and ran them around her areolas, the circles dark through her flimsy gown. Her nipples grew hard and prominent through the thin fabric.

Alex smiled, imagining sucking on those luscious bits of her. *Soon, soon,* he promised himself.

In the office Violet tugged open Nick's belt and unfastened his pants. Nick's cock sprang out, fully erect. She went to her knees in front of him and licked the head, then drew the whole thing into her mouth. Nick's eyes closed and his head fell back, his breath deepening, matching time to Violet's movements.

Outside the doorway, Echo stared and she put her fingers into her mouth, attempting to mimic what Violet was doing to Nick. Alex's smile widened at her efforts. She was getting pretty good at it. He couldn't wait to test out her expertise on his own cock.

Speaking of which...watching the couple and the spying nymph was making his penis ache for attention.

Well, what would be the harm? As quietly as he could, Alex unfastened his pants and slid his erection out. He stroked himself with a far too practiced hand. It felt good, but not nearly what he knew Nick was feeling. Self-reliance had its limits. If only he could convince a handy mythical nymph to give him pleasure.

The mythical nymph in question had transferred her moistened fingers to the cleft between her legs, clutching her gown with her spare hand to get it out of the way. She worked her fingertips up and down her woman's folds, lingering in the sensitive spots. To Alex it looked like she was as practiced with this kind of self-pleasure as he was...and as frustrated by it.

Well, he had a fix for that, something he would propose just as soon Nick and Violet finished their little session, when Echo would head back to her statue. He had a plan that would leave both of them satisfied.

In the room, Violet's skirt came off and Nick slid her underpants down her thighs, past the stockings and garter belt she still wore. Stockings and a garter belt...Alex grinned. For a woman with as innocent a demeanor as Violet had, she sure knew how to dress to please her man. Nick's face registered delight as he slid his hands up and down the silky fabric covering Violet's legs.

Lifting her onto the edge of the desk, he spread her thighs and moved between them. The look on Violet's face was pure love as Nick drove his cock deep within her. The pair moaned loudly, fortunately drowning out the matching moans of Echo and Alex as their fingers sped up to match the now furious pumping of Nick into Violet.

Under his hand Alex's cock spasmed and his release grew imminent. He slowed, holding off. He didn't want to finish this way, coming in his hand while watching the woman he desired masturbate. Shaking, he carefully replaced his still aching cock into his pants and zipped them up.

Echo leaned against the wall, her fingers delving deeper into her pussy, seeking elusive sexual relief. Violet and Nick moved in well-practiced unison, knowing just what tricks to pull to give each other the ultimate pleasure. Violet nibbled Nick's neck, while he lifted her ass off the table, driving deeper into her. She shuddered and let loose a sharp cry into his neck. He clutched at her, once, twice, then a deep groan erupted from him as he emptied himself into his wife.

At the doorway, Echo cried out as well, a pitiful sound after the joyful noise that Violet had made. She might have found some relief, but Alex knew it hadn't been sufficient. Her face registered frustration as she wiped her fingers on her gown.

Still joined, Violet and Nick leaned together, talking in quiet whispers, their faces radiating love for each other. For a moment Alex watched, drawn by the sight of their intimacy. That's what sex looked like when love was involved. Even in the good days with Mel he'd never had that.

Alex shook his head and stared in the other direction. He wasn't looking for love, didn't want a lover, certainly didn't want to be part of a couple like Violet and Nick. The last time he'd gotten serious about a woman...well, thinking about it wouldn't do any good. Some wounds took a long time to heal, and he wasn't ready to deal with the ones Mel had left behind.

All he wanted was a woman to ease his aching balls, to satisfy his need for a good fuck. Echo was just the woman he wanted—beautiful, with great legs and tits, and she needed satisfaction as much as he did. She couldn't leave the museum and follow him home, wouldn't expect more than what she got from him. When they finished they would part company, no muss, no fuss.

Echo also watched the happy couple cuddling and whispering sweet words to each other. Straightening, she leaned against the doorframe and waved her hand. The door reappeared, solid as it had been. For a moment she stood still, her look defeated, then slowly she moved down the hallway back towards her statue.

Her attitude radiated sadness, and Alex felt a momentary pang of sympathy. She looked like she'd loved and lost someone just as he had. Maybe what he had in mind wasn't such a good idea...he could wind up hurting her, and that wasn't right.

Then again...Echo needed to get laid as much as he did and he wanted her too much to give up. He'd try to convince her to have sex with him. If she refused, so be it, he'd let her go. But if she didn't refuse…it was too tempting to not try.

Keeping out of sight, he followed her.

As she reached the narrow hallway leading to the gallery that held her statue, Echo walked faster and Alex had to run through an adjacent room to get in front of her. He had to be between her and her statue, but they needed to be beyond earshot of Violet and Nick for his plan to work. He arrived at the end of the hall just as she appeared at its other end. He held his breath as she came towards him.

When she reached the middle of the hall, he deliberately cleared his throat. Immediately Echo froze in place and pressed against the wall, her eyes frantic as her gaze searched the darkened hall.

Alex moved out of the shadows and into the hall, moving to within a few feet of her startled form. He tried a reassuring smile that got no response from her other than a further widening of her green eyes.

Well, it was now or never. "Hello, Echo. Having fun?"

Watch for NEMESIS OF THE GARDEN, the next in the Divine Interventions series, available Fall 2004.

About the author:

Cricket Starr lives in the San Francisco Bay area with her husband of more years than she chooses to count. She loves fantasies, particularly sexual fantasies, and sees her writing as an opportunity to test boundaries. Her driving ambition is to have more fun than anyone should or could have. While published in other venues under her own name, she's found a home for her erotica writing here at Ellora's Cave.

Cricket welcomes mail from readers. You can write to her c/o Ellora's Cave Publishing at P.O. Box 787, Hudson, Ohio 44236-0787.

Also by Cricket Starr:

The Doll

Why an electronic book?

We live in the Information Age—an exciting time in the history of human civilization in which technology rules supreme and continues to progress in leaps and bounds every minute of every hour of every day. For a multitude of reasons, more and more avid literary fans are opting to purchase e-books instead of paperbacks. The question to those not yet initiated to the world of electronic reading is simply: *why?*

1. *Price.* An electronic title at Ellora's Cave Publishing runs anywhere from 40-75% less than the cover price of the exact same title in paperback format. Why? Cold mathematics. It is less expensive to publish an e-book than it is to publish a paperback, so the savings are passed along to the consumer.
2. *Space.* Running out of room to house your paperback books? That is one worry you will never have with electronic novels. For a low one-time cost, you can purchase a handheld computer designed specifically for e-reading purposes. Many e-readers are larger than the average handheld, giving you plenty of screen room. Better yet, hundreds of titles can be stored within your new library—a single microchip. (Please note that Ellora's Cave does not endorse any specific brands. You can check our website at www.ellorascave.com for customer recommendations we make available to new consumers.)

3. *Mobility.* Because your new library now consists of only a microchip, your entire cache of books can be taken with you wherever you go.
4. *Personal preferences are accounted for.* Are the words you are currently reading too small? Too large? Too...**ANNOYING**? Paperback books cannot be modified according to personal preferences, but e-books can.
5. *Innovation.* The way you read a book is not the only advancement the Information Age has gifted the literary community with. There is also the factor of what you can read. Ellora's Cave Publishing will be introducing a new line of interactive titles that are available in e-book format only.
6. *Instant gratification.* Is it the middle of the night and all the bookstores are closed? Are you tired of waiting days—sometimes weeks—for online and offline bookstores to ship the novels you bought? Ellora's Cave Publishing sells instantaneous downloads 24 hours a day, 7 days a week, 365 days a year. Our e-book delivery system is 100% automated, meaning your order is filled as soon as you pay for it.

Those are a few of the top reasons why electronic novels are displacing paperbacks for many an avid reader. As always, Ellora's Cave Publishing welcomes your questions and comments. We invite you to email us at service@ellorascave.com or write to us directly at: 1337 Commerce Drive, Suite 13, Stow OH 44224.

Printed in the United States
20871LVS00005B/1-72